KONOSUBA:
GOD'S BLESSING ON THIS
WONDERFUL WORLD!
7
110-
Million
Bride

Aqua
Darkness
“Hey, is this woman with the disgusting light you’re talking about…me?”

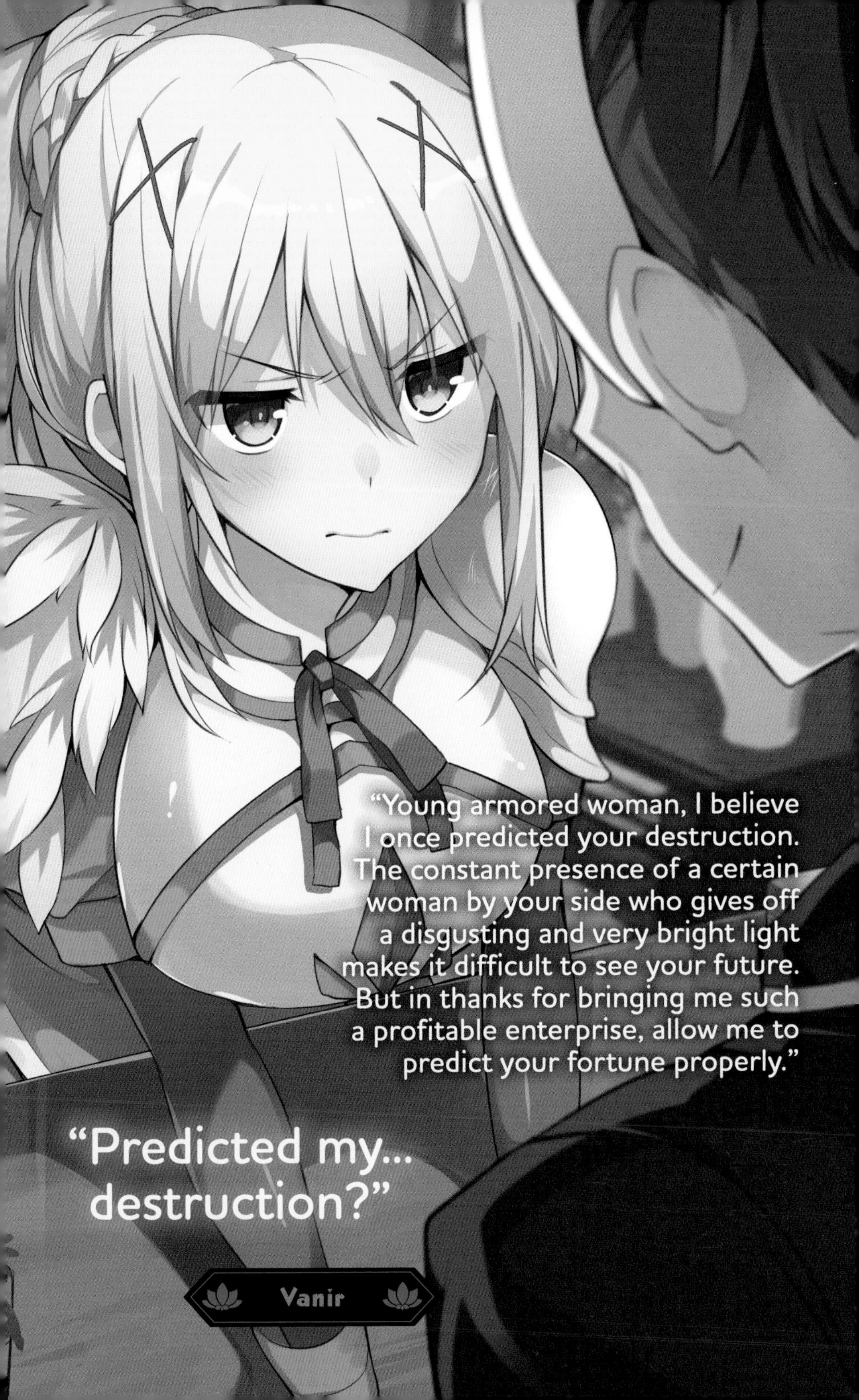
"Young armored woman, I believe I once predicted your destruction. The constant presence of a certain woman by your side who gives off a disgusting and very bright light makes it difficult to see your future. But in thanks for bringing me such a profitable enterprise, allow me to predict your fortune properly."
"Predicted my... destruction?"
Vanir

"*This* time
I shall earn the
nickname
Dragonslayer!"

Megumin
"Let me go home! Pleeease let me go home! I've got the worst feeling about this!"

"K-Kazuma!
Kazuma, let go!
Let go of me!"

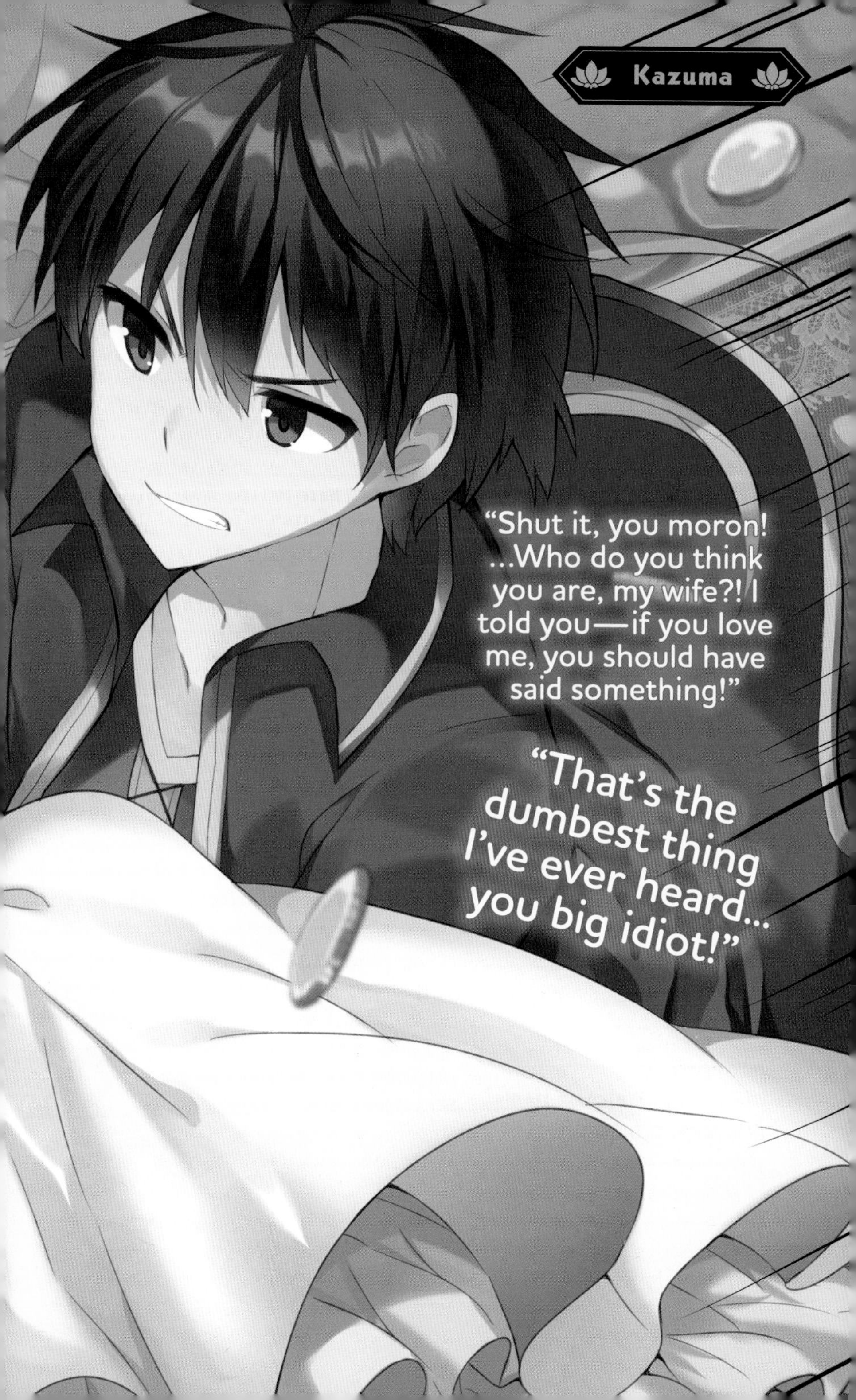
Kazuma
“Shut it, you moron! ...Who do you think you are, my wife?! I told you—if you love me, you should have said something!”
“That’s the dumbest thing I’ve ever heard... you big idiot!”

KONOSUBA: GOD'S BLESSING ON THIS WONDERFUL WORLD! 7

110-Million Bride

CONTENTS

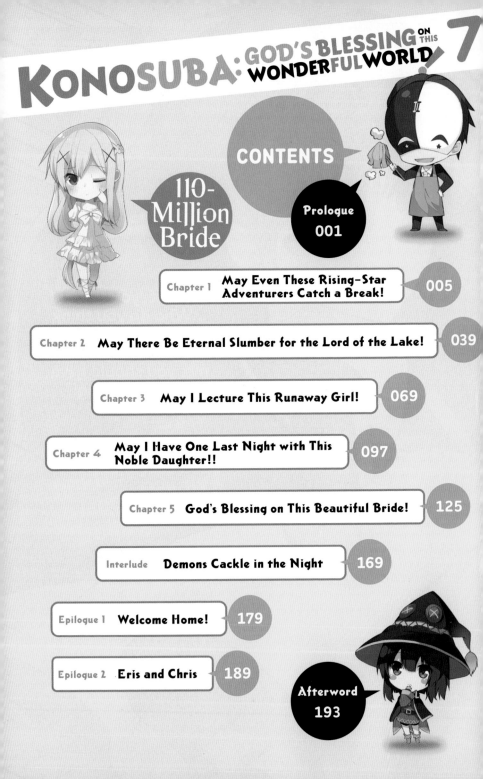

KONOSUBA: GOD'S BLESSING ON THIS WONDERFUL WORLD!

110-Million Bride

7

NATSUME AKATSUKI

ILLUSTRATION BY

KURONE MISHIMA

YEN ON

NEW YORK

KONOSUBA: GOD'S BLESSING ON THIS WONDERFUL WORLD! 7

NATSUME AKATSUKI

Translation by Kevin Steinbach
Cover art by Kurone Mishima

This book is a work of fiction. Names, characters, places, and incidents are the product of the author's imagination or are used fictitiously. Any resemblance to actual events, locales, or persons, living or dead, is coincidental.

Yen On
1290 Avenue of the Americas
New York, NY 10104

Visit us at yenpress.com
facebook.com/yenpress
twitter.com/yenpress
yenpress.tumblr.com
instagram.com/yenpress

First Yen On Edition: December 2018

Yen On is an imprint of Yen Press, LLC.
The Yen On name and logo are trademarks of Yen Press, LLC.

The publisher is not responsible for websites (or their content) that are not owned by the publisher.

Library of Congress Cataloging-in-Publication Data
Names: Akatsuki, Natsume, author. | Mishima, Kurone, 1991– illustrator. | Steinbach, Kevin, translator.
Title: Konosuba, God's blessing on this wonderful world! / Natsume Akatsuki ; illustration by Kurone Mishima ; translation by Kevin Steinbach.
Other titles: Kono subarashi sekai ni shukufuku wo. English
Description: First Yen On edition. | New York, NY : Yen On, 2017– |
Identifiers: LCCN 2016052009 | ISBN 9780316553377 (v. 1 : paperback) |
ISBN 9780316468701 (v. 2 : paperback) | ISBN 9780316468732 (v. 3 : paperback) |
ISBN 9780316468763 (v. 4 : paperback) | ISBN 9780316468787 (v. 5 : paperback) |
ISBN 9780316468800 (v. 6 : paperback) | ISBN 9780316468824 (v. 7 : paperback)
Subjects: CYAC: Fantasy. | Future life—Fiction. | Adventure and adventurers—Fiction. |
BISAC: FICTION / Fantasy / General.
Classification: LCC PZ7.1.A38 Ko 2017 | DDC [Fic]—dc23
LC record available at https://lccn.loc.gov/2016052009

ISBNs: 978-0-316-46882-4 (paperback)
978-0-316-46883-1 (ebook)

10 9 8 7 6 5 4 3 2 1

LSC-C

Printed in the United States of America

KONOSUBA: GOD'S BLESSING ON THIS WONDERFUL WORLD!

110-Million Bride

Characters

Darkness
Age 18
Job Crusader
A female knight who specializes in defense and enjoys being beaten up by monsters. Daughter of the Dustiness family, a powerful noble house. Special skill: fantasizing.
Aqua
Age Unknown
Job Arch-priest
A goddess who gives guidance to the young and deceased. Goes to a parallel world with Kazuma to defeat the Demon King. Likes wine. Special skill: party tricks.
Megumin
Age 14
Job Arch-wizard
Exceptionally talented, even by Crimson Magic Clan standards. Obsessed with the überpowerful spell Explosion, she is neither capable of nor interested in using any other magic. Favorite thing: Explosion. Special skill: Explosion. Hobby: Explosion.
Yunyun
Age 14
Job Arch-wizard
Vanir
Age Unknown
Job Terrible Demon, Shopkeeper
Kazuma Satou
Age 16
Job Adventurer
An adventurer and *hikikomori* (in any world) who brought Aqua to their current plane. Has already given up on defeating the Demon King.
Chris
Age 15?
Job Thief
Eris
Age Unknown
Job Goddess

Prologue

"You impossible—impossible—*impossible* man! Why do you always have to be like this?!"

"Me?! Why do *you* always have to be like this? I'm the only one you ever get this angry with! What is it about me that ticks you off so badly? Wait—are you trying to get me to notice you? Like some kind of hot-cold type? If you're in love with me, just say so already!"

I fired my retort at Darkness from the sofa, where I was lounging on my stomach. Her eyebrow arched dangerously.

"And just what makes you think I would ever fall in love with a layabout virgin shut-in like you?! That's the dumbest, stupidest thing I've ever heard, and I'm not afraid to let you know it!"

"Aww, leave me alone! This is my special ring-polishing time! I got this ring from Iris! If I lose it because we were fighting, what am I gonna do then? This thing's irreplaceable, you know!"

This was of particular concern to me because at that moment, Darkness had me by the collar.

"That's exactly why I'm so upset about this! It's a national treasure that was with Princess Iris every waking moment until she gave it to you. You can't polish it with a dirty handkerchief!"

"That hurts! Even I have my pride, you know. I admit this handkerchief isn't the fancy kind, but I am taking care of it in my own way. This ring is precious, the touchstone for all my memories of Iris!"

"You think I'm worried about how much that rag cost?! I've seen you blow your nose on it! Go get a nice new polishing cloth this instant!!"

With that last belligerent shout, she finally put me down again. A second later, she collapsed onto the couch herself, looking drained.

"Sheesh. Being around you is the most exhausting thing," she said. "We're finally back home, and I can hardly even relax."

"*You* can't relax? It's practically your hobby to cause trouble for me, and you think you can stand there and lecture me? I know you only barely qualify as upper-crust, but you *are* supposed to be a blue blood, right? It wouldn't kill you to act just a little more refined and, you know, noble."

"'Only barely'?! The Dustiness family, the house people call the kingdom's confidant, 'only barely' noble?! In the whole wide world, I think you're the only man who could insult me so thoroughly!"

"Look, if you're trying to compliment me, you're not doing a very good job. You need to be clear and precise when praising someone."

"I'm not praising you!" Darkness leaned back against the sofa and took a sip of the black tea sitting on the table. "I know, I know. You've always been this way. Even when I told you who I really was, you cared less about my background than my name. You're weird that way."

"Whoa, what's this, Lalatina? You of all people have no right to call me weird. A sheltered rich-girl-cum-adventurer-cum-masochist? You want all the archetypes you can get your hands on, don't you, you greedy lady?"

Darkness set the tea back on the table. "I can see I'll have to settle things with you eventually."

"Yeah, sure. Let's have us another duel sometime, *my lady*."

She looked regretful, but I didn't pay much attention to her. Instead, I also picked up a cup of tea and took a sip. "Hey, this is pretty good. Despite all the things you suck at, you make a pretty mean cup of tea."

That seemed to placate Darkness a bit. "Heh-heh! People don't tend to think much of my cooking, but I'm confident in my tea-making abilities. The trick to a good cup of tea is warming up the mug first, then pouring the tea out to the last drop. If you apologize for the nasty things you said to me, I might see my way to making you another cup."

"Okay, okay. I'm sorry for teasing you. Tell you what—to make it up to you, when your household falls into disgrace, I'll hire you as my maid."

"Disgrace?! Sheesh. You really are hard to fathom. Just when I think you're a lazy good-for-nothing, you show a bit of courage. Sometimes you help people out, and sometimes you spend all night partying with the weirdest crowd and doing all sorts of other things I can't approve of. For goodness' sake, which one is the real you?"

"The real me? Whatever. Everyone does the occasional good deed when they're in a good mood. But then they get a little upset, and suddenly they're peeing on a wall somewhere. I'm just a normal person like that. Sorry I'm not the big-shot, serious hero you wanted."

"Hmm? You don't have to be sorry. I like average guys better than princes or heroes or whatever. Guys just like you…"

"H-hey, what're you implying? What are you trying to say? First Megumin, now you—what is it with you girls and these ambiguous declarations? How's a virgin supposed to understand you if you don't speak clearly?"

My words only brought a thin smile to Darkness's lips. "Hmm. Now, what *do* I mean…?"

And then she sipped her tea, looking rather pleased.

Chapter 1 May Even These Rising-Star Adventurers Catch a Break!

1

The letter summoning us to the Adventurers Guild arrived a few days after we had gotten back to Axel.

“Now then, Adventurer Kazuma Satou. Regarding the matter that led us to bring you here…”

One of the Guild’s front-desk girls was holding a heavy bag and beaming at me.

“…as the amount this time is so large, it’s taken us a while to get the money together. However, here is your reward for the defeat of the Demon King’s general Sylvia—three hundred million eris! This makes *four* generals of the Demon King you’ve vanquished, Mr. Satou! You’ve become a real veteran of our guild! Please accept this reward!”

“““““““Ooooooh!”””””””

There was a cheer from the gathered adventurers. Smiling generously, I reached out for the bulging sack, which was indeed very heavy.

“Hey, you guys, take it easy. You act like I’ve never taken out a major bounty before. Three hundred million eris is hardly worth all this ceremony… Huh? Um, Miss, you can let go of that bag anytime now.

I've got a good grip on it—I won't drop it. Hey, c'mon! Leggo! G-get your hands off that!"

The guild girl seemed loath to part with the money.

The building echoed with the murmuring of adventurers.

"Man, Kazuma and that party of his have taken down four generals! When they started out, I wondered how long it would be before they all got slaughtered. But look at them now!"

"Yeah, no kidding. They couldn't even manage a few frogs before, and now Kazuma is one of the richest men in Axel. Some things just don't make any sense."

"Hey, I've always said Kazuma is a guy who comes through when it counts."

"Weren't you the one who said we should take bets on how long it would be before his party got wiped out? Well, it doesn't change how impressive they are. Kazuma's an Adventurer; they're supposed to be the weakest class. He's got zilch in the way of equipment, and he *still* goes toe-to-toe with the Demon King's generals!"

I had finally managed to wrest the money away from the guild girl and started hugging it protectively. I looked around at the peanut gallery whispering about me.

Keeping my face as straight as I could, I said, "Gosh. You think you're going to get anywhere with flattery like that?"

Then I exclaimed:

"Well, you're right! I'm ordering a round of the finest wine in the house for everyone here!"

"Yeaaaaaaah! Ka-zu-ma! Ka-zu-ma! Ka-zu-ma!"

"Yessss! You're wonderful, Kazuma! Marry me! And then take care of me for the rest of my life!"

"Best nouveau riche in Axel!"

"That's Nothing-but-Luck Kazuma for you!"

"Ha-ha-ha! Praise me all you want, guys, but you won't wheedle anything else out of— Hey! Who called me Nothing-but-Luck Kazuma? I have all kinds of things besides Luck!"

It had been close to a year since I came to this place. It was a long time coming, but it was finally here:

My moment.

"You're the worst! Kazuma, you are the worst! Here I am, sick with worry because you're late getting home, and then I find out you're secretly having a party without me? I was right to come and check on you!"

Aqua was sitting across from me at the Guild, which was 20 percent noisier than usual.

"Look, I'm sorry for staying out so late, but you were the one who said that when our party gets summoned to the Guild, it's always bad news, and sent me here by myself. Oh, hey, look. Here's a nice cold Crimson Beer. Come on, have a drink."

I took the Crimson Beer that I had ordered for myself and set it in front of Aqua.

"Hey," she said, "if you think a little alcohol is all it takes to get rid of me, you've got another think coming. Megumin was wandering around the house like an angry bear, muttering, 'He still hasn't come back…' every five minutes. And Darkness kept holding her head and exclaiming, 'Was it because of what happened before?! Surely Lady Iris must have realized who the thief really was! Argh, what am I gonna do?!' …*Glug, glug.* Ahh! Say, bring me another Crimson Beer!"

Aqua downed her drink in a single gulp, so excited she was practically pounding the table. Another beer was swiftly ordered.

Beside me, Megumin took little sips of her drink and said, "Still, I'm glad to know we were summoned for something good for once. Aqua said we should have a wager about whether the news would be good or bad. She wanted to bet three thousand eris that you had committed some awful crime and were being held in detention at the Guild right about now."

Hey.

"Then she said we should get our stuff together so we could make a quick exit if it turned out you'd gotten caught up in some kind of trouble," Darkness added. "I can prove it. Just check out that backpack by her feet."

As Aqua merrily ordered another beer, I inspected the contents of her pack, then lit into her.

"You jerk, acting like you were all worried about me! What's with this backpack?! Hey, that next Crimson Beer is mine!"

"No way—get your own! And it's true I was a *little* worried! Think how hard my life would be without you! Like…! Okay, well, what about…? I mean, there's always… Huh? Hey, Darkness, remind me what problems we would have if Kazuma disappeared."

"You unbelievable jerk! Do you have any idea how much I put up with from all of you?! I'm about ready to strangle you—how's about we step outside?!"

"Hey, what do you think you're pulling on, you boor?! You'll stretch my divine raiment out of shape! Stop it! Stop it already!" Aqua beat at my hand, which was clutching a fistful of her feather mantle as I tried to drag her out the door.

Beside Aqua, Darkness took a long sniff of her wine and said tiredly, "Gosh. What Lady Iris saw in such a brutish and immature man, I'll never know… Maybe it was his exotic appeal, plus a touch of temporary insanity…"

A lot had happened in the capital. Some other adventurers and I had repelled an attack by the Demon King's army, and I had protected the nobles of the city from a thief. I had even saved the entire country from a near crisis, although nobody knew it. And above all, I had gained an adorable little sister named Iris…

"I wonder how Iris is doing anyway?" I mused. "I worry sometimes that she spends her nights weeping from loneliness… Oh, I know! I'll ask Vanir to make a doll that looks just like me. He said his Vanir dolls that laugh in the night are a big seller. How about a Kazuma doll that laughs in the night? I could send it to Iris, and then she wouldn't have to be lonely."

"Don't you send her any bizarre gifts like that, Kazuma! Stick to letters. I can have my messenger deliver them. Try anything else, and you might be branded a terrorist and thrown in jail!"

2

And so a week passed after I received my reward from the Guild. We had done nothing but travel recently, and it felt good just to stay in Axel for a while.

"Hey, who made this?! Find the chef who cooked this and tell them that Kazuma Satou, super-rich adventurer who is currently the talk of the town because of how rich he is, is asking for them!"

"Yeah! And tell them the Arch-priest Aqua is asking for them, too!"

With our newfound wealth, Aqua and I had quickly become patrons of Axel's finer dining establishments, enjoying gourmet meals on a daily basis.

A young man I took to be the chef came over to the corner of the restaurant we had claimed as our territory.

"I-is anything the matter, honored customers? Is there a problem?" He was practically shaking at the abrupt summons.

"Oh, no," I said. "This meal is exquisite, and I just wanted to thank you personally. I spent a fair amount of time in the castle in the capital recently, and I'm impressed that you managed to please even my discerning palate."

"Th-thank you very much, sir," the chef said, bowing to us.

Aqua wiped her lips with her napkin and said, "I'll bet the secret ingredient in this stew is wine, correct? This richness could only come from red wine. I would say…thirty-year-old Romanée-Conti. Yes?"

"It's just vinegar, ma'am. I got a special deal on it earlier."

"Goodness. Who knew one could extract such fine flavor from cheap vinegar? Excellent work."

"Oh, how gracious. Thank you very much." The chef bowed to Aqua. Now that he knew we weren't going to yell at him, he had regained his composure.

While the chef stood there smiling, I brandished a piece of meat on my fork at him. "The stew was good, but what really got my attention was this. This softish stuff. If I had to compare it to something, it would be… Hmm. Sneaking into the room of a girl you like, your heart pounding, and opening her closet only to discover it's a Mimic. It's got that powerful impact, the sort of thing that throws you off balance. You understand what I'm saying, my good chef?"

"Not a word, sir."

"I see. Well, the point is, this is absolutely delicious. The Adventurer Kazuma Satou gives this restaurant three stars."

"I also give this restaurant three stars," Aqua added.

"Thank you so much," the chef said with a broad smile. "I'll do my best to make this shop worthy of four stars in the future."

I gave him several eris bills. "Ha-ha, that's what I like to hear! It was delicious. We'll be by another time. These bills represent our appreciation for a fine meal. Keep the change as a tip. Thanks again."

"Yes, thanks!" Aqua said.

"Exact change. Well, we hope to see you again anyway. Thank you very much!" The chef remained upbeat as he saw Aqua and me out of the store.

This was how I had spent the days since becoming a newly minted rich man with Sylvia's bounty: living in the lap of luxury. We'd split the 300 million among the four of us, and as for me personally, I had even more cash coming to me because of my business deal with Vanir. I had enough now that I never needed to work again for the rest of my life, even if I splurged a little.

Talk about life's winners. I had struggled and slaved and had finally joined the ranks of successful adventurers.

Patting our bulging stomachs, Aqua and I went back to our house, a mansion fit for top-class adventurers like us. We were happily discussing where to go for dinner as we opened the door…

"We're ho—"

"Argh, you are one unbelievably perverted Crusader! Here, this is what you want, isn't it? Stop putting on a brave face. Just cry uncle and I'll— Oops."

"You think this can break me? On my pride as a Crusader, I can do this for an hour, or two hours, or— Oh!"

We found Darkness, curled up in a bedroll and left in the foyer, and Megumin, crouched before her and dangling some ice in front of her face teasingly. Both of them were red in the face as if from heat, and Darkness was panting heavily.

Our eyes met. I quietly closed the door.

The door burst back open, and a flustered Megumin came flying out.

"Please don't close the door! This is not what it looks like, you two!"

"No, hey, don't worry about it; we understand. Aqua and I will go have a nice meal out, so you guys just keep doing what you're doing. We can even find somewhere else to stay tonight."

"The Axis Church recognizes homosexual love, you know. Do you need a magical blessing?"

"You don't understand at all! Let me explain! Darkness is—"

Megumin grabbed both of us by the arm and dragged us desperately inside.

"Grr!" Darkness growled. "You're going to mount a humiliation assault on me, too?! You think just having Kazuma and Aqua see me in this highly compromising position is going to get me to give up?!"

"Your incessant chatter is *not* helping our case, Darkness! Pipe down!"

I was only briefly distracted by Darkness, who was still making a scene from her entrapment on the floor. I noticed I could feel heat leaking out from the open door.

It was almost summer, but these two had lit a fire in the fireplace.

"This isn't some perverse game," Megumin said. "Darkness asked me to help her work on strengthening her endurance. She claims that she wins this town's annual Endurance Championship every year." Flushed, she held the ice out toward the equally red-faced Darkness.

"I don't know whether to be relieved or disappointed," I said. "But if you're going to practice this stuff, do it at Darkness's family's house or something. Don't turn our living room into a sauna."

Darkness let out a relieved breath as Megumin pressed the ice against her and said, "Actually, my father hasn't been in such good health lately. If he found me doing anything like this at home, he would worry about what his unmarried young daughter had been up to. I'm keeping it here out of consideration for him."

"You sure he didn't get sick because you kept piling logs on the fire at his house?"

Having the ice pressed against her seemed to have calmed Darkness down and drained some of the weird tension in the air. "Phew...," she said. "With you and Aqua home, maybe it's time for me to come clean. With Megumin's help, I've found that, since my level is higher than last year, my resistance to heat has improved as well. I'm sure I'll take the crown again this year. Hey, Kazuma, could you let me out of here?" She shifted pointedly in the bedroll.

......

"You remind me an awful lot of my predicament when I got hit by Bind back at Alderp's mansion."

Darkness looked at me questioningly. "I do? Come to think of it, I guess something like that did happen. Well, we can talk about it later. Come over here and set me free. I'm soaked with sweat under this futon. I want to hurry up and take a bath."

Aqua and Megumin, fully aware of what I was saying, crouched down next to Darkness. They were both grinning.

Darkness looked at us, unease finally showing on her face. I made a show of waving my fingers at her. "We've been together a long time, Darkness. Surely you know what I'm like by now. For example, whenever I've been wronged, I always return the favor. Now then, Darkness. I recall that when I was immobilized back in the capital, you weren't

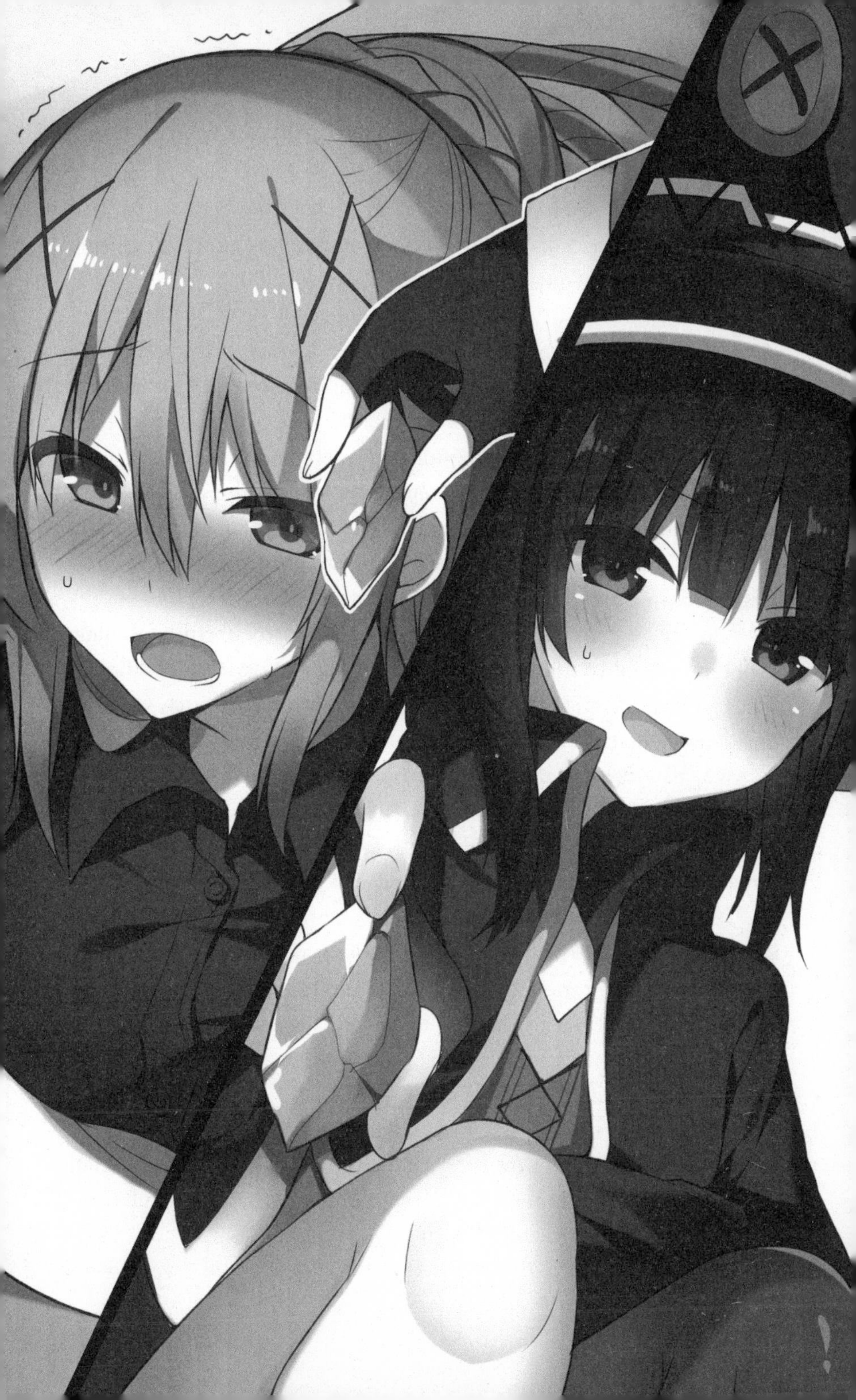

afraid to abuse me. And what an interesting position you find yourself in now!"

"Hrk! J-just kill me!"

Her face flushed once more and she started struggling to escape. That was the first knightly thing I'd heard her say all day.

"Phew… Kazuma really had his way with my hot, helpless body."

"H-hey, watch how you say things! It sounds really dirty when you put it like that."

The lot of us had tickled Darkness into submission together.

She may have been making me sound like a total perv, but Darkness looked pretty pleased overall. "I was hoping to practice some more tomorrow," she said. "Kazuma, maybe you could be the one who dangles the ice in front of me while I try to endure the heat?"

"No way… I *said* no way. Stop looking at me so hopefully." I made a shooing motion at Darkness, who put on her best disappointed face.

I looked at Aqua, who was sitting barefoot on the couch with her knees drawn up to her chest.

"Gosh, whatever happened to the proud, assertive Darkness from the capital?" she asked. "Look at me. Just last night I went and purified the souls in the town's common graveyard. I contribute to society like that every day. You should learn from my example."

What had actually happened was that Aqua had completely forgotten her promise to Wiz that she would periodically purify the cemetery, and when rumors started up recently that ghosts had been causing more trouble than usual, she had rushed to go and take care of it.

Oh well. No need to bring that up now. There was something else that had been bothering me even more than that.

"What's that thing you've been holding to your belly?"

Aqua had a blanket over her knees, on top of which was a small egg. When we went out together, she would forever have her hand in her pocket, playing with it.

"Ohhh, curious, are we, Kazuma? Very well, let me tell you. Listen and be amazed—this is a dragon egg!"

""A dragon egg?!"" Megumin and I exclaimed together.

Aqua, looking very pleased with herself, said, "The other day when I was looking after the house by myself, this traveling merchant showed up. He'd heard of us and was very impressed. 'What an honor to meet you!' he said. 'I've been looking for adventurers just like you—the type who can face down the Demon King's army and live to tell the tale! The kind who sneer at danger and battle the Demon King day and night! I have a special gift for you!' He said if we were going to keep on battling the Demon King, we would at least need a dragon, and I thought that made sense."

He had "heard of us"? Something smelled extremely fishy here. I had a feeling what he had "heard" was that we had a lot of money.

Aqua went on about her dragon egg, totally oblivious to the sour look on my face.

"Now, listen. I'm aware you're a know-nothing who's totally ignorant of the ways of this world, Kazuma, so let me enlighten you. Dragon eggs are extraordinarily difficult to come by. When one does arrive at the market, it's always snapped up by a noble or some rich guy. So when someone specifically seeks you out to sell you one, what else can you do except buy it? This is a dragon we're talking about. A dragon! Isn't that exciting?"

It would be a lie to say the thought didn't pique my interest, but the more I heard, the fishier this sounded.

"And how much was this egg you bought?" I asked.

"You're not going to believe this. He said everything I had would be payment enough. Dragon eggs usually go for at least a hundred million. When I asked him why he was willing to part with it for so cheap, you know what he said? He told me that unlike nobles and rich people, who just wanted to buy status, powerful adventurers would raise this dragon so it could be part of the coming battle with the Demon King!"

She cradled the egg lovingly in her arms. I got a bit of vertigo.

"And you…bought it?"

"Of course I did. I've even named it already. His name will be Zeltman Kingsford. And I'm going to be his mother, so you can rest assured that one day he'll be a ruler among dragons! You can feel free to call him Emperor Zel."

As Aqua spoke, she bathed the egg she was holding in a soft light. Was she using magic to keep it warm? Or was this how a goddess helped speed up a creature's growth?

It didn't really matter, because from every angle, this appeared to be a chicken egg.

"Anyway," Aqua said, "I won't be taking part in any quests until he hatches. I really can't take my eyes off the little guy, so Kazuma, could you bring my dinner here?"

I thought a fried egg would make a perfect side dish for dinner tonight.

3

"Okay, we're heading out. Sorry to stick you with doing such a stupid thing, Megumin."

"I don't mind. Anyway, if we don't do this, Aqua will never go outside, and say what you might, she's the only one who can deal with that demon."

The following day.

I headed for Wiz's shop with Aqua and Darkness in tow. Megumin was staying home.

She had lit a fire in the fireplace, even though it was plenty hot outside; spread out a blanket in front of it; and was keeping Aqua's egg warm. This was my concession to the goddess, who had flatly refused to leave the house while she was busy trying to hatch her egg.

The two girls and I arrived at a cozy little magic-item shop tucked away off the town's main street.

Despite the early hour, Aqua began pounding on the door. "Let us in! Please! Come on—open the door! The sun is already up and everything! Your best customers are here! Hurry and open up shop!" It was true; we were certainly familiar faces around this place.

After Aqua's commotion, a series of stomps could be heard from inside, and then the door burst open.

"Is there no time of the day when you're not noisy?! Think of the trouble you're causing to the neighborhood! You're a threat to public order! We're not open yet, and we won't be for a while! Go wash your face and then come back."

This tirade came from a part-timer in a bizarre mask—the lackadaisical demon Vanir.

"We're not here as customers today. We've got something else in mind!" Aqua shot back. "You guys are always busy when you're open for business. We got up especially early to come here and talk to you, so you should be grateful. Come on—let's hear it! Say thank you!"

She gave a triumphant little snort as she faced down the demon.

It so happened that this store's main business at the moment was selling items I'd invented, and it was making them a lot of money. I had taken my payment in a lump sum in exchange for the intellectual property rights, so however much product Wiz's shop might move, I wouldn't see any more cash. Still, as the inventor, I was certainly happy to see my ideas being so well received.

"You're renowned for your inability to read a situation, and I'm not pleased by your insinuation that you've done me some kind of favor. I assume there's a punch line to that remark. But never mind. I know what you're here for. The newly rich boy wants his reward. Come in and wait; I'll get it for you."

With that, Vanir went into the store, but Aqua stuck to him like glue, saying, "Be grateful! You can say: 'Thank you so much for taking your precious time to come visit a worthless excuse for a demon like me.' Go on—say it!"

"You expect me to ever say such a ridiculous thing?! Our tired-from-pulling-so-many-all-nighters shopkeeper is sleeping in the back, so keep your voice down! If you insist on continuing to besmirch the name of our shop with your antics, I'll put a curse on you that will make aloe grow from your behind!"

"Just you try it! A curse from a shrimpy little demon like you would never have any effect on me. Are you stupid? You said that mask is your true body—I guess there's no room in there for a brain."

"Bwa-ha-ha-ha-ha-ha-ha! Bwaaa-ha-ha-ha-ha-ha-ha-ha! Clearly, we need to settle things between us. Very well, I suggest we take this outside!"

They began to swipe at each other, and I pulled them apart. "Okay, I need you guys to stop fighting every single time you so much as look at each other. Anyway, what's this about Wiz pulling a bunch of all-nighters? Is the store really that busy?"

"Indeed," Vanir replied, "this is precisely what they mean when they speak of laughing all the way to the bank. We sell our stock as quickly as we can make it, so the owner neither rests nor eats but spends her days minding the store and her nights producing more to sell. This cycle has gone on for nearly two weeks now, and she has reached a point of emotional instability. She'll break into laughter or tears for no particular reason. She's in no position to receive customers, so I'm having her take a rest."

"Y-you…" I could hardly believe what I was hearing.

Vanir returned with a bulging sack in one hand. "I was thinking to myself: How do I take a shopkeeper who inevitably gets into trouble when left to her own devices and keep her from steering right back into the red? I've been observing her, and I noticed that when she has too much free time, it leads her to do unwise things. So I hit upon the idea of keeping her busy twenty-four hours a day, without so much as time to eat—and I must say, it's worked rather well."

He handed me the bag even as the repugnant comments came out of his mouth. Wiz might be an immortal Lich, but he could at least let her rest every now and then!

Hey… Exactly who was the shopkeeper and who was the employee here anyway?

"Incidentally," Vanir said, turning to Darkness, "you, the one who's been idling there this whole time. The one whose body burns with sexual desire, night after night, despite being a virgin."

"Whaaa—?!" Darkness shouted and practically came flying at Vanir. He dodged her easily.

"Mm, yes, negativity dripping with the utmost embarrassment, delicious. Young armored woman, I believe I once predicted your destruction. The constant presence of a certain woman by your side who gives off a disgusting and very bright light makes it difficult to see your future. But in thanks for bringing me such a profitable enterprise, allow me to predict your fortune properly."

Then he gave an ugly and fittingly demonic smile.

"Hey, is this woman with the disgusting light you're talking about…me?" Aqua said, grabbing Vanir's shirt.

"Predicted my…destruction?" Darkness said, frowning. Before she could go any further, I jumped in.

"Hey, forget about that. Give me some more details of what you were saying about Darkness a minute ago!"

Tears beading in her eyes and face red up to her ears, Darkness decked me.

4

My teeth were still rattling when Vanir said, "Very well, then, let me look. O girl who has a pronounced yet strange sense of duty as a noble but lacks the abilities to back it up, and therefore spends all her time in fruitless effort, it is well that you've come here."

"……"

Darkness sat across from Vanir, saying nothing and chewing her cheeks in apparent distress. As I watched her, I rubbed my face where Darkness, on the brink of tears, had punched me. Aqua said I had reaped what I'd sown and refused to cast Heal on me, so I tried to reduce the swelling with Freeze.

I still intended to hit up Vanir later and find out what he'd been getting ready to say about Darkness.

"I'm telling you, Darkness, take a demon's predictions with a large grain of salt," Aqua said. "I guarantee my pure and precious prophecies would do you more good than anything you'll hear from a weirdo like him."

I highly doubted that.

"Hmph. My prophecies are not like those of the gods, half-formed and to be interpreted in any way one pleases. I am the all-seeing demon and second to none in my vocation. Now then, I'm going to ask you some questions. Some may be difficult to answer, but try to be honest."

"O-okay… But I'm a paladin of the Eris sect. Why do I have to get my fortune told by a demon all of a sudden?"

"Well, it's free, for starters," I said. "All you have to do is answer some questions, right?"

Darkness murmured her agreement and then straightened up, facing Vanir.

"Mm, it seems you're ready," he said. "Then, first, place your hand atop this crystal ball. Good, now all you need to do is wait. Please answer my questions honestly."

"Er… R-right…" Darkness had her hand on the crystal ball as Vanir had instructed.

"Now, I ask you. A Crusader needs both defense and enough weight to dive into the fray, yet you've been assiduously lightening your armor of late. Why is that?"

The question caused Darkness to tremble with surprise. "W-well, I…I th-th-thought, since I'm so clumsy, if I made my armor lighter, maybe it would be just a little easier for me to hit something… J-just a l-little…" Darkness faltered with nearly every syllable.

"I told you to answer honestly," Vanir whispered.

……

"I noticed I've been getting more and more muscular lately, so I decided to…lighten my armor…" She was looking at the ground in embarrassment, and her voice was so soft it wouldn't have drowned out the buzzing of a housefly.

Wait, Darkness was getting ripped?

And that bothered her?

Vanir nodded with satisfaction when he heard this.

"Very good. Now, I ask you. The dress belonging to your wizard friend that was left in the laundry basket in the bath. You secretly held it up to your body, looking at yourself in the mirror and muttering happily, 'Yeah, no way this would work. No way…' Why was that? Further, why was it that while you spoke, your usual joyless, brusque countenance lit up with a smile? And why did you then blush, take a look around, and then quickly return it to the basket?"

He wasn't kidding about being all-seeing.

Just how much can you tell me, my honored Vanir?

"C-c-cute clothes don't look good on me, and I would be embarrassed to buy any or have any bought for me, so I've never touched them before… I just noticed it there and thought maybe I'd try it on… It was just the passing impulse of a brusque, hyper-muscular girl. Forgive me… I'm s-s-sorry…"

She covered her red face with both hands, apologizing profusely in a shaking voice. I didn't really think holding up Megumin's clothes against herself demanded that kind of apology, but it looked like after having her foibles called out like this, Darkness was watching her ability to resist go down to zero.

"A cute dress? You should do it, Darkness! You're always wearing cool stuff or grown-up stuff. You even wore a fancy one like a real noblewoman that one time. So what's wrong with adding something adorable to your wardrobe? We would never hold it against you that you secretly try on cute clothes!" Aqua, no doubt totally devoid of any malice, pumped her fist encouragingly.

This was too much for Darkness, who was already hiding her head in her arms against the table; she went red up to her ears.

Vanir nodded in distinct satisfaction at this display. Then he said, "Finally, then. You continue to wear clothes that expose your figure, even though you know that young man you live with can't stop looking at you with carnal lust. Why?"

"What—?! What in the world does this have to do with telling my fortune?!"

Darkness, looking like she was about to cry, pounded her fist on the table.

Vanir gave her a genuinely puzzled expression.

"When did I say I needed you to answer these questions in order to tell your fortune? I only said I was going to ask them. As far as telling your future, placing your hand on the crystal ball is enough. The interview is just to kill time until the fortune comes out, and I— Hey! Hey, stop that! How can you touch my mask so easily? Stop weeping and trying to pull it off!"

Darkness had her hand on the crystal ball again, but she refused to look at any of us, no doubt upset about having been duped. Vanir was peering into the crystal orb.

"Oh my. Mm. Yes, that *would* lead to a prediction of destruction. Your house, and your father, is in for some trouble soon. And you, dim as you are, will take an impulsive action in the belief that if you sacrifice yourself, it will make everything better. But your deed will not make anyone happy. Your father will spend the rest of his life in regret and gloom. Avoiding this fate is—"

Darkness's face became progressively more serious as Vanir spoke.

"Oh. Impossible, with your strength. When the moment arrives, your best fortune will come of leaving everything behind and fleeing. Get a fresh start in a place far away with this man who is thinking, 'With the right push, I could probably convince Darkness to fulfill all my desires' yet lacks the courage to cross that line, fearing your current relationship will not endure."

"All right, hold on. Every time you open your mouth, my party members trust me less."

Darkness stood without a word. I flinched, but she didn't seem angry. I mean, why would she be? I only thought a push might get me somewhere. I hadn't actually done anything yet.

"Vanir," Darkness said. "Thanks for the reading. But if I end up in a crisis like the one you've mentioned, I won't be able to run away. I'll listen to some of what you have to say, though. Kazuma, you've got lots of money now, and you obviously don't intend to go on any quests for a while. Not that I'm especially worried about this 'fortune,' but it's been a while since I've been home. Maybe I'll go see my dad."

Then Darkness left the shop.

5

"Listen to me, you third-rate demon. Can't you say anything more specific? You were the one complaining about how vague the gods' prophecies are. And do a reading for me, too. At least tell me what kind of dragon Emperor Zel is gonna be when he hatches. Tell me if he'll have what it takes to rule over the other dragons. Oh, and I used all my money to buy Zel, so I need you to tell me a quick and easy way to get more. Surely the all-seeing demon knows that much, right?"

After Darkness left, Aqua tried to wheedle favors out of Vanir, but he only frowned with distaste.

"I have never encountered such a vulgar goddess. If there were such an easy way to make money, I would have let my wreck of a shopkeeper in on it, and I would currently be using the proceeds to set up my dungeon. My powers allow me to see what a person has done in the past and what's likely to befall them in the future. If they're used merely to satisfy greed, little good is likely to come of them. You don't even seem to realize *that*. Are you truly a goddess?"

That provoked a snort of laughter from Aqua. "Even for a demon, that's blatant false advertising. Geez, you're worthless! Let's go home, Kazuma. I want to get back to hatching Zel. The sooner he's born, the sooner I can start him on an all-demon diet."

"Oh-ho, something's coming to me," Vanir said. "Your Emperor Zel. You'd best change his name to Terry. Terry Yaki! Then he'll be much beloved, especially at the dinner table!"

Vanir and Aqua stood, sort of laughing together.

"My, my, wherever did you get a name like that? You know what hatches from eggs, don't you? Dragons! I paid a lot of money for that egg, so why would I give him a name that sounds like food?"

"I, the all-seeing demon Vanir, stake my very fame on this declaration: What emerges from that egg will be an excellent physical specimen, as you judged—excellent for his delicious meat!"

I decided to leave the two of them to their glaring contest. I stood up, clutching my reward protectively. I would deposit it at the bank, to keep it from being stolen or lost.

The influx of cash put me in good spirits, and I was just about to walk out the door, leaving the supernatural enemies to stare daggers at each other, when—

"Wait, boy who is pleased to have come into even more money and is excited about his overnight reservation at the 'usual place.'"

I stopped in my tracks. You know, I really wished he would stop snooping into where I had reservations.

"Do you remember what I told you when we first ran into each other at the shop?" Vanir asked.

"What do you mean? Did you tell me something?"

Hey, how long ago was that? Was I supposed to remember all that time ago?

"O boy who, having a memory no better than that of a goddess, forgets the advice I went out of my way to give him. I suppose it can't be avoided. I shall give you a new piece of advice. You would do well not to be content with the payment you've received but to make plenty more things to sell. You believe you won't want for money again, don't you? I told your Crusader friend earlier that her strength would not avail her, did I not? But with your strenuous efforts, it may yet."

"*I'm* going to give you some advice, too. The money you've worked so hard to save shall be reinvested with Wiz, and after a short while it will all be gone! ...Well? What do you think? The all-seeing Aqua has told your future!"

"".........""

Wiz's shop still rang with the sound of shattering potions, two bickering voices, and more stuff breaking as I left to head home.

Along the way, I mulled over what Vanir had said at the end. He had predicted that Darkness's family, along with her dad, would come to grief. Darkness would impulsively sacrifice herself to help, and how it ultimately turned out would depend on me. And finally, he'd told me to keep coming up with new products if I wanted things to work out for her.

...What the heck was he talking about?

6

It happened a number of days later, when I had thoroughly forgotten about Vanir and his prophecy. The door burst open without a knock, and an unfriendly-looking man in a butler's outfit bustled in without so much as a by-your-leave.

"I apologize for disturbing you at this time, and indeed during a meal. I have urgent business with the lady Dustiness that brings me here. May I request a moment of her time?"

The man didn't even give his name but only bluntly announced his business, appraising us (we were busy eating) with cold eyes.

Darkness, who did not look very happy, left a vegetable speared on her fork as she responded, “You refer to me as Lady Dustiness? Then you must be the servant of some noble family. I suppose I can deign to hear you out. What do you want?”

“Indeed,” the man murmured, and then, “My master, Alderp Barnes Alexei, has requested your immediate presence. Out of consideration for where you’re living, a carriage is waiting outside. The details will be conveyed at my master’s residence. If you would follow me, please.”

To refer to a person’s beloved home as simply “where you’re living” was awfully rude, but it didn’t seem to bother the man as he gestured toward the door. I could hear the fork creak in Darkness’s hand as she squeezed it so hard it bent out of shape. I was worried that my impulsive noblewoman of a friend would haul off and hit him, but she only set the twisted utensil on the table.

“I’m going out for a while,” she said. “If I’m late coming back, lock the front door. I’ll see you later.” Then she followed the man outside, leaving the rest of us to wonder what had just happened.

“Who was that? And what did he want?” Aqua said.

“He mentioned Alderp. He’s that old noble goon, isn’t he? I sure hope she’s not getting herself caught up in anything weird again.”

We went quiet, our faces downcast, collectively hoping that nothing unpleasant was about to happen.

“If Darkness isn’t staying, then I can have her leftover hamburger, right? You’ll feed it to me, won’t you, Megumin? Kazuma is the worst at feeding people. Yesterday he was feeding me some soup, and he tried to put it right up my nose!”

Quiet, that is, except for one person who couldn’t read a room to save her life nor use her hands because they were still wrapped around her egg.

The next morning.

“It’s summer already; isn’t it time for you to shed some of this fur?

You know, you don't act much like a cat. How do we get you to go back to your real form? I mean—that's it, isn't it? You're secretly a beautiful cat-eared girl who adds *meow* to everything she says, just hiding in the body of a cat, right?"

I was sitting in the warm sunlight by the living room window and brushing Chomusuke, who was perched on my knees. I had been keeping up a steady stream of banter for a while now. So far, though, I hadn't been able to get any response.

Every once in a while I got the impression that Chomusuke could understand human language, but I still hadn't gotten her to reveal who or what she really was.

The only thing I was sure of was that she was not a normal cat. Meaning that if this were a manga or something, she would definitely turn into a beautiful woman at some point, but…

"Just so we're clear, I don't have anything against beautiful nonhuman women. It doesn't matter what you are, okay? You always come crawling into my bed on cold days. If I woke up one morning to find you had turned into a girl, you can bet I wouldn't panic. Wouldn't even move. Of course, no matter what you are, you're welcome to stay in this house as long as you like, so don't worry. In fact, we'll cook some nice fish for you every day."

At the mention of fish, Chomusuke, who had been sitting there and enjoying being brushed, looked up at me with a twitch of her nose.

"Aha, I see that got a rise out of you, you little gourmand. Okay, Chomusuke, listen up. If you turn into a person, your body will be bigger, meaning you'll have more room for fish. See what I'm getting at?"

"Mrrrow," Chomusuke answered, then purred and batted at my hand as if to demand more brushing.

"Okay, you're pretty cute. Stay cute, all right? Even if you do transform into a person one day. Please don't turn out to be a loser heroine like the rest of this bunch. If you behave, I promise you'll get a taste of that chicken we're expecting."

Then I started brushing again. Suddenly, the door flew open.

* * *

"Kazuma! Let's hunt a monster with a huge bounty on it!"

Speaking of loser heroines, the one who had worried us all by not coming home the night before was back now, first thing in the morning, and spouting idiocy the moment she opened her mouth.

"You're doing the walk of shame, and this is the first thing you say? I don't care where you were or what you were doing with whom, but you aren't married yet, so try to keep the prodigal-daughter act to a minimum, okay?"

"The walk of *what*? I was out so long last night that I thought I would just bother you all by coming home so late, so I went to my family's house! But more to the point!!"

Darkness came over and thrust a piece of paper at me.

"Have a look at this!"

"Bounty monster," I read. "Kowloon Hydra? What kind of hydra is that? Is it like Yamata-no-Orochi, the many-headed snake monster?"

The paper Darkness had given me boasted an illustration of the creature in question, along with a detailed description of its behavior and habitat. I looked at the flyer unhappily; Darkness cocked her head at the name Yamata-no-Orochi.

"The Kowloon Hydra lives in the mountains near Axel," Darkness said. "It's a big-game monster that spends most of its time fast asleep. When it uses up all the magical power it's stored in its body, though, it goes to sleep at the bottom of a lake and starts absorbing MP from the surrounding land. An especially large hydra can take up to ten years to store enough MP to wake up again, and this one last went to sleep just about a decade ago."

In other words, it was due to be awake again soon. Looking at the description on the paper, the word that came to mind was *big*. I mean size-of-a-house big.

As if that wasn't scary enough, its name and appearance made it look like the final boss of some video game.

"You got up so early, your brain hasn't caught up with your mouth yet. We're not hunting this. What was that butler on about last night anyway? Megumin was worried, you know. You don't have an ounce of street smarts, and she thought we shouldn't send you off with some random noble."

"F-forget about last night! It doesn't have anything to do with any of you. If you don't want to get involved with the nobility, then keep your nose out. And where is Megumin? I think she would be very interested in this quest."

"Megumin went out with Aqua. They were going to find a cool collar for the dragon they're expecting."

"Yeah, Aqua asked me to help her build a hutch for the dragon when he's born, but that egg sure reminds me of…" She glanced at me awkwardly, like she couldn't quite bring herself to say it.

"No matter how you look at it, I'm pretty sure it's a chicken egg," I said. "But whatever. I'm not going on this little quest of yours. You and Megumin and Aqua can all go together. But if you come crying back to me like you always do, don't expect me to help."

"When have I ever come crying back to you?! …Actually, just the other day I heard a report that the lake looked kind of weird. You know that wasteland around it? They say some bushes are growing there. That's got to be because the hydra has stopped drawing magical energy from the area. It's a sign that it's about to wake up!"

Darkness stopped, then resumed in a dramatic tone.

"You hear me, Kazuma? The only ones who can save this town are the ones who have already defeated general after general of the Demon King—our party! If you're any kind of adventurer, then you'll want to protect our home! Kazuma Satou, Hero, Vanquisher of Countless Generals of the Demon King! Your city needs you now!"

Darkness issued this exhortation with her fist balled and her eyes gleaming, but I just laughed.

"Do you think I'm stupid enough to go rushing out just because you called me a hero? We've known each other longer than that. You know the kind of stuff that motivates me to get involved in an adventure. And by the way, it's not money. I've got plenty of that now. But I'm sure you can think of a few other things."

Darkness looked downcast at this. At last, blushing slightly, fist still bunched up, she said, "O-okay. I understand. The day we defeat the Kowloon Hydra, I'll give you a reward that should utterly delight you. A k-kiss on the cheek—"

"You idiot. What are we, kids? You think I'm gonna risk my life for a kiss?"

"?!"

Darkness had really worked herself up to make this offer, and my flat refusal took her by complete surprise.

"You know what makes me angriest of all?" I said. "The fact that you even think one measly kiss is worth all that much. What's with this self-confidence of yours anyway? I know the nobles in the capital made a big deal over you, but don't get carried away, all right?"

"Wh-wh-why, you…!" Darkness began to tremble uncontrollably. I picked up Chomusuke and looked her in the face.

"Hey, Chomusuke. Can you believe this girl? She actually thinks one little kiss is gonna convince a guy to risk his life. Don't you think there's a better way to handle this situation?"

"Meeeow," Chomusuke replied.

"Oh, you do? I do, too! All kinds of better ways, really."

"You son of a—! You have some nerve! Put down that cat so I can kill you!" Darkness's eyes were bloodshot and her fists were at the ready, but I made a show of stroking Chomusuke, enjoying the sensation of her fur on my fingers.

"Hmm? Not just stupid but a one-trick pony, too. You think your physical strength is going to help you? Remember, I've got the Bind skill now. I can tie you up in the blink of an eye. Of course, if you *want* to go back to Tickle Hell, then be my guest!"

I smiled maliciously, but for some reason Darkness blushed a little.

"Bind? Yes, I suppose I am aware that you've learned how to make good use of that skill. V-very well. Let's have a little contest. If you can manage to tie me up, then you can do whatever you want to me, just like you did the other day. But if you think I'll be intimidated by a bit of rope, you're wrong!"

"Why do you look happy about this?! Forget it. There's no reason I should go, is there? If you want to go, take Megumin along. The monster shows up, she drops an Explosion on it, and you're done, right? If that doesn't do the trick, you can just run away. 'Hydra' sounds like a subspecies of dragon. I bet it's covered in tough scales. A feeble Adventurer like me couldn't—"

I stopped midsentence. Not because Darkness was angry or because she was attacking me. Instead, she had gone completely silent and gloomy, and I found myself lost for words.

Was she really so eager to kill this monster?

"A-are you absolutely sure you won't help me?"

She knelt on the ground in front of me and gazed at me with tremendous sadness.

The old break-down-and-cry method. You know, maybe she *had* learned something about how to get what she wanted.

7

About a half day's journey south from Axel was a small mountain. We arrived at the foot to find a lake spreading out before us, the water a muddy green color.

"Hey," I said, "come to think of it… What do we do if we can't defeat the hydra? If our attacks don't work on it, then worst-case scenario, we've taken a monster who was being perfectly quiet and ticked it off."

"No! Noooooo!" Aqua cried.

Darkness, however, answered, "Don't worry about that. Whenever there's been trouble with a Kowloon Hydra in the past, the military came out and surrounded it and just let it rampage until it ran out of

MP and went back to sleep. Given the current circumstances, I expect a detachment of knights from the capital should be showing up anytime."

"Noooo! I don't want to deal with any hydras! Why are you so interested in this reward anyway, Darkness? Was Kazuma right? Is your family really that poor? Let's go home! I'll smash open my piggy bank and lend you some money! Please let that be enough!"

I see. So even if we screw up, there will still be a bunch of knights to cover for us.

"I take it the problem is that the hydra woke up earlier than expected," I said. "And even if those knights can put the thing back to sleep, they won't be able to actually kill it, so it doesn't solve the root problem at all. That's why they wanted me, the defeater of so many powerful foes, to come and help."

"Let me go home! Pleeease let me go home! I've got the worst feeling about this!"

It seemed to me that if help was on the way, it would make sense just to wait for them and then work together to defeat the monster. Why was Darkness in such a hurry to slay this hydra?

It was then that Megumin, practically bubbling with excitement, removed the patch from her eye and laughed.

"Bwa-ha-ha-ha-ha-ha! Shall I have you leave things to me this time? A subspecies the hydra may be, but it's still a variety of dragon! When I destroy it, I can boldly proclaim myself Dragonslayer! My desire for this sobriquet once led me to explode a wyvern, another type of small dragon, but for some reason—perhaps because I was just a child—it was not counted among the monsters I've defeated. *This* time I shall earn the nickname Dragonslayer!"

"When Emperor Zel hatches, we'll have a dragon in the house—and you want to be known as a person who kills them?! Hey, Megumin, let's drop this! I'm sure Zel would never let you ride him if you were a dragon slayer. Come on, come home with me!"

I nodded at Megumin's brave declaration, then looked out into the middle of the lake.

"Okay, then. First we have to—"

"I need to hurry home and watch to see when Zel is born! Waaaaaah!"

I finally got sick of Aqua's incessant whining. "Don't you ever shut up?! It takes at least twenty days for a chick to hatch; you've got plenty of time! Now give it up already. If you leave, how are we going to wake the hydra?"

"Why do you think a chick would hatch from a dragon egg? And why did I have to leave my precious Emperor Zel somewhere like *that* anyway?" At the moment, Aqua's egg was at Wiz's shop.

"What were we going to do? There's no one else stupid enough to take us up on just watching an egg to see if it hatches. If we asked any of the adventurers we know, they would probably have eaten it by the time we got back."

Having said that, I did notice Wiz drooling a bit when we dropped the egg off with her.

"But! But! I'm afraid leaving poor Zel with a Lich and a demon will have a weird effect on him! Dragon parents spend a long time carefully nursing their eggs, you know. It helps the children gain exceptional magic power or take on their parents' elemental affinities! I want my little Zel to be born a holy White Dragon. What if their dark powers get to him and he comes out as a Black Dragon instead?!"

"Then you would end up with a black-colored chick. If you're that worried about it, then help us beat down this hydra in a hurry so we can all go home. If Megumin's magic doesn't do the trick, we won't have many other options aside from getting the hell out of here."

I must have finally convinced Aqua, because she calmed down a bit. Darkness drew her great sword.

"All right," she said, "everyone ready? Get us started, Aqua!"

The plan was brilliantly simple. Most water-dwelling monsters hate pure water. That meant an opportunity for Aqua's normally bizarre and useless powers.

"Okay, fine. Not that I object to purifying water as such. I'll be right back, then! If Megumin's explosion doesn't work, we run right back home, okay?"

Then, as quick as a wink, she jumped into the murky lake. She swam around, splashed, flopped a little.

Watching from shore, Megumin muttered, "Is that how purification works? She's not just playing in the water because she's hot, is she?"

She was right; from where we were standing, it looked a lot like some kid just playing around, but I was pretty sure this was exactly how the plan was supposed to go.

We looked on as Aqua, perhaps tired from purifying such a large lake, closed her eyes and just floated on the water.

"Hey, Kazuma," Darkness said. "Aqua's taking a nap right over where our monster is sleeping. Is that safe? Speaking of which, I've always wondered—how is Aqua able to purify water like that without even doing a chant or anything?"

"She claims it's because she's a water goddess," I said. As usual, though, both of the other girls seemed to let this possibility go in one ear and out the other.

As we chatted, the breeze blew the water goddess ever closer to the middle of the lake. It was probably a little late to be wondering if we should have attached a string to her or something.

The three of us had stopped feeling so anxious about the surreal scene, even yawning a little, when it happened. A few small ripples ran across the surface of the lake. Megumin had started to nod off, but now her eyes snapped open.

"Oh…! It's here! Here it comes! I feel an incredible magical power! It's coming from the bottom of the lake!"

No sooner had she spoken than a massive shadow appeared underneath Aqua, who was still asleep. Something very, very large was floating to the surface.

"How long do you plan to nap for, Aqua?! Wake up! It's right beneath you! Megumin can't let off her spell with you floating there!"

My shouting woke up Aqua. She started treading water with

remarkable facility for someone who had been asleep just a moment before. She yawned and looked around. Then, finally grasping the situation, she started swimming toward us in a hurry.

"Hey, that thing's a lot bigger than we were told!" I called. "The flyer said it was the size of a large commoner's house—but that thing's bigger than our mansion!"

As the shadow in the lake grew larger and larger, Darkness's and Megumin's frowns got deeper and deeper. The whole size-of-a-house thing was what had made us think Megumin might be able to handle it with her Explosion. But at this size, there was no way a single strike was going to do it in.

"K-Kazuma! Kazumaaaaa! Something reeeeally big is coming right for me!"

The shadow finally became a recognizable silhouette, eight heads clearly visible beneath the water. And all of them were reaching for Aqua!

"Here it comes! Megumin, get the boom ready! Darkness, take up a guard position in front of her, just in case! I'm going to keep back and make sure we have an escape route ready!"

"Leave the protection to me! But there aren't any other monsters around, so I don't think we need anyone to secure an escape route!"

"It's a b-b-bit b-bigger than I imagined, b-but I'm s-s-sure my explosive firepower can take care of it in one shot! I'll fry every living thing in this lake!"

"I don't care what you fry—just do it! Do it!"

As we ran around in confusion, the creature appeared.

Ahh…

All my success recently had led me to underestimate these big-game bounties.

The eight heads and eight long necks came rising out of the lake, dripping water.

"—! —!!"

* * *

The hydra's howl, a sound beyond description, cut through the air. It wasn't even all the way out of the water yet, and it already looked like a small island.

Staring vacantly at the heads leering down at me from high in the sky, I muttered:

"I think we'd better forget this one."

Chapter 2 May There Be Eternal Slumber for the Lord of the Lake!

1

"O Kazuma! Death should not have taken thee!"

I found myself in an all-too-familiar white room. As I opened my eyes, I saw that the upbeat voice belonged to Eris. She could be surprisingly saucy. And actually, she seemed to know a lot about Japan.

"...You're in high spirits, Lady Eris."

"Sorry. It's just that everybody says that, and I wanted to try it once." She gave me a mischievous wink. To see a real goddess, with her unearthly beauty, do something so cute was practically enough to make me hyperventilate.

Next, however, she scratched her cheek and looked a bit distressed. "Still, Kazuma, getting sent here doesn't even seem to faze you anymore. Let's see... Your friends are all okay. They've escaped the hydra and gotten somewhere safe. As far as your corpse, Darkness deliberately got herself eaten by the hydra and somehow managed to retrieve it."

Now, this was a goddess who knew what she was doing. She had calmed all my fears before I even had a chance to voice them.

"Deliberately got herself eaten? God, she doesn't know when to quit, does she?"

After the monster had woken up, we'd somehow collected Aqua, and then Megumin had let loose with her Explosion.

Which was great, as far as it went.

"I don't think that's very fair, do you?" I found myself complaining to Eris. "Growing back its lost heads? I mean, really?"

That's right: Megumin's blast blew off several of the hydra's heads, but it magically regenerated them and then went on as if nothing had happened.

There was another question, too…

"What kind of shape is my body in after being eaten by a hydra? I'm pretty sure I can't be resurrected if the injuries are too extensive…"

And that would be the end of me.

"Let's…see… Yes! It's all right! You can be resurrected! Only about thirty percent of your body is missing. That should be workable!"

Maybe I would have been happier not knowing.

"…G-great…!" I wilted a little.

Eris looked at me pleadingly. "When you get back, don't be too hard on Darkness, okay? I know she was the one who pushed you to fight this monster, but…she had her reasons—I promise. So… She's absolutely racked with guilt over your death; she's really in shock. Not as much as you, having just died and all, but still…"

She looked very worried as she tried to console me.

………

She really is a sweetheart…

I tried to think. Did I have anyone like this in my life? Wiz? Yunyun?

No, they were both very nice, but Lady Eris gave me this overwhelming sense of security, like an embrace.

"Don't worry—I won't shout at her," I said. "Say, Lady Eris, you told me once that you occasionally come down to the mortal plane to have a little fun. Do you ever happen to come by Axel? I'm always a little sorry that the only time we get to see each other is when I've just died…"

Eris held back a giggle. "We've met each other repeatedly in the mortal realm. I think it's about time you put two and two together.

Honestly, I'm a little disappointed that you haven't yet." She sounded so teasing.

...Wha...?

"Wait, what did you just say? That I *have* met you? You mean, like, in Axel? Wha...? What?"

Even with this little hint, I couldn't quite seem to grasp it. I had already met her? Repeatedly?

When? Where? Who had I seen who might fit the bill?

Watching me fret, Eris couldn't hold back a little laughter.

"Okay, let me give you a clue. Down there, I don't look the way I do now. I'm a little more lively, and I don't even speak exactly the same way."

A different appearance, livelier, and a different way of speaking...?

"And I may be a goddess, but don't use Aqua as a point of reference—not all goddesses end up as Arch-priests..."

I hardly let her finish before I exclaimed, "Oh, I've got it! You're Maris, aren't you? The one who broke Keith's nose when he was all, 'I guess it's true that the size of an Eris priest's chest is inversely proportional to her faith!'"

Eris started laughing again. "No, I'm afraid not."

Huh?

No, wait, it has to be—!

"Seris! The one who teamed up with Darkness to give Dust a beating after he was like, 'I heard the goddess Eris pads her bra—I bet an Eris priest with big boobs would be in for some divine intervention! Are those even real? If you two aren't using padding, you'd better prove it to me right now—off with those shirts!'"

"Wrong again." Eris was still smiling, but I thought I could sense a hint of anger, too.

But if she wasn't Maris and she wasn't Seris, then who...?

Just as I was starting to sweat, Aqua, with her impeccable ability to spoil a moment, started shouting:

"Kazuma! Kazumaaaa! The resurrection's all set! Hurry up and get back here! Darkness is really depressed, and she smells funny! Come on—hurry up!"

It bugged me a little that Darkness was feeling down, but I had more important things to attend to right now.

Having said that, I was also totally out of ideas. "Lady Eris, I give! I give up; I'm sorry! Please tell me the answer; I'm begging you! Otherwise, what if I accidentally do something rude to you without knowing it and end up incurring your wrath?"

Eris looked like she couldn't quite decide what to do. "Something rude? Wrath? I think it's a little late to be worrying about that, after what you did to me the first time we met..."

"Huh?"

"Nothing, nothing. My true manifestation is a secret." She pointed meaningfully at herself. "And while we're at it, don't believe everything my senior goddess says to you, okay? I'm not w-wearing any pads, at least not right now!" She patted her chest for emphasis, blushing just a little.

Then the white door I knew so well appeared in front of me. I started to panic slightly. She still hadn't told me who she was on the mortal plane!

Completely ignoring my plight, the door began to open, a bright light shining from within...

"H-hey! Lady Eris, I'm sorry! I didn't mean to make you mad! I didn't mean for you to sulk! I honestly don't care about the size of your chest, I swear!"

"Farewell, Mr. Kazuma Satou! I certainly hope the next time you see me here, you'll have figured out who I am. Bye-bye, now! Have a safe trip!"

Eris's cheeks were still red, and she refused to tell me the answer to the bitter end. But the crimson color in her skin made me notice something: a white line on her right cheek.

"Huh? Lady Eris, there's something on your ch—"

I didn't get to finish my sentence before she shoved me through the cold, unfeeling gate.

2

"Welgome bag, Gazuma!"

I opened my eyes to see Aqua holding her nose.

The reek that suddenly assaulted me caused me to jump to my feet.

"Holy—! It stinks in here!"

There was a sour, fishy smell, and it was coming from…

"Me?! Is my body making that stench?!"

I guess when you spend enough time in the stomach of a hydra, you start to smell like it.

Then something else dawned on me: No one would meet my gaze. And that, in turn, led me to another revelation. I was stark naked.

"My clothes dissolved, huh…?"

"Yes, they did. Would you cover yourself already? Anyway, Kazuma, there's so little of you left that we should call you Kid-zuma for a while. Your armor is done for. That sword of yours, the one with the weird name—it's still here, but the scabbard is gone."

"I shall not stand idly by while you belittle the name I bestowed upon that sword!"

Megumin was all over Aqua. I ignored them, taking up the bare katana that was left.

"And what are you so upset about?" I asked.

Darkness was over in the corner with her knees up to her chest, looking downcast; she smelled as bad as I did and was no more popular because of it. She shuddered when I spoke and looked at me apologetically.

"Aren't you angry with me for forcing us into that fight?"

"Why the heck would I be angry with you? Yeah, you were the one who was all excited to go for it, but it's not like we aren't used to fighting the Demon King's generals and big game…or me dying."

"That's true, I guess…" This seemed to throw the normally straightforward Darkness off her rhythm.

"That wasn't like you," I said. "I heard from Lady Eris how you got yourself eaten by the hydra just to help me. Heck, I can see you've got blood specks here and there. Are you okay? You don't look too dissolved."

Darkness glanced at me. "This blood splattered on me after I rescued you. I had to cut my way out of the hydra. Much longer in there, and I would have suffocated and perished as well. But I'm okay now. I'm not injured."

She still looked pretty bleak.

"I appreciate your going in to get my body," I said. "Thanks. Hey, come on, let's hurry home and take a bath. Sound good?" I smiled as if to say, *No worries, right?*

"Hey, Kazuma, I'm glad you're trying to cheer up Darkness, but I don't think you should be offering her a bath in that state."

Oh, that's right. Naked. Oops.

3

"I finally understand why the royal knights haven't offed that hydra yet. It's not that they won't; it's that they can't."

We were on the road back to Axel, reflecting on the battle with the monster. We practically had to drag Darkness, who still seemed depressed about something.

"Apparently, a Kowloon Hydra uses all that magic to regenerate lost heads," Megumin said. "To defeat it, one would need to hit it with such immense firepower that it would be unable to regenerate, or otherwise to wound it over and over, forcing it to use up all its magic regenerating, and then finally deal it a mortal blow when it was out of MP. Neither seems very practical…"

She was right about that. And hydras weren't stupid. You could keep on hurting it, but that was why it fled to the bottom of the lake to regenerate its MP. As for firepower, what could we use that would be more powerful than one of Megumin's explosions?

I looked back at Darkness, who was trudging along at the tail of our formation. "Megumin's right," I said. "This one's too much for us. Let's just let the knights deal with the hydra. They can work down its magic until it goes to sleep. You okay with that, Darkness?"

After a long pause, "Yeah" was the only answer we got.

Had she really been that interested in taking out a big bounty?

Then Aqua spoke up, looking inordinately pleased with herself for some reason. "Well, it's not all bad news. Thanks to me, that hydra won't be coming out of that lake anytime soon! It'll consider the water I purified to be an infringement on its territory, and it'll be busy polluting the lake again. That should buy enough time for the knights to arrive and take care of things."

"Hold on a second," I said. "What's this? Did you actually do something worthwhile? Something almost…clever?"

The two of us were ecstatic, but Megumin, riding on Aqua's back, offered, "When Aqua is this confident, there's usually a catch."

Why did she have to go and jinx us?

I was normally the one to give Megumin a piggyback ride after she had used up her MP, but today she asked Aqua to do it, claiming I smelled funny.

"No, no, I don't think there'll be any trouble this time," I said. "Heck, even if there is, it won't be our fault. We were the ones who bought some time for the knights to get there!"

"That's right!" Aqua added. "Do you have some problem with the way I work? I can't believe you, Megumin! You'd better be nice, or I'll make you ride with Kazuma or Darkness."

"Please, anything but that! I apologize!"

We got back to town without any special trouble.

"Megumin and I will go report to the Guild. You two stink bombs should go home and take a bath. The way you look right now, Kazuma, you'd probably just get arrested anyway."

At the moment, I was covered in nothing but a cape I had borrowed from Megumin, and between that and the smell, I was eager not to attract too much attention.

"Let's go, Megumin! Be sure to exaggerate what we did as much as possible. We can't get a reward for killing the monster, but maybe we can score some cash!"

"Just leave it to me! I shall spare them no detail of the impressiveness of my Explosion!"

Somewhat against my better judgment, I let the two of them go, and Darkness and I headed back to the house.

4

Once we were home, I let the still-gloomy Darkness take the first bath, then I went in and soaked until the smell was finally gone.

"It's kind of scary what a person can get used to," I muttered to myself as I sank into the tub. "I just died, but it doesn't especially bother me." I looked down at my body, about a third of which had been destroyed. Aqua had joked about calling me Kid-zuma, but I had been healed back to my, uh, original size, right?

There in the bath, I did a thorough inspection of the parts of me that had gone missing.

I heard Darkness's worried voice from the changing room. "Kazuma, you're taking even longer than usual in there today. Do you hurt? Or are you still trying to recover your physical strength after coming back to life?"

"I-I'm just fine! No problem! That smell was awful, right? I'm just making sure it's all washed off."

Darkness was kind enough to be concerned about me despite her own depression. I could hardly tell her that I was making sure I hadn't "shrunk" after having my body restored.

In spite of my assurances, Darkness didn't go anywhere. She was just standing there. Was there something she wanted to say?

After a moment, she managed to come out with, "Hey, Kazuma. I'm… I'm sorry I forced us into that hunt. Everything's gone so well for us in the past, I guess I just got overconfident. I really wanted to take down that hydra."

"Well, I think we've seen the last of it anyway," I said. "All's well that ends well. What's taking Aqua and Megumin so long? I bet they stopped at the Guild for a nice meal. Let's hurry over and catch up with them there."

"Y-yeah… Sounds good…" Darkness still didn't seem very happy.

…Was there some kind of connection between that hydra and her? Or did it have something to do with that butler from the other day?

"I left you a change of clothes in here, okay? I'll be waiting in the living room."

She was about to leave the changing room.

"Is there some reason you feel like you have to defeat that hydra?" I asked.

"?! W-well, I…!"

Bingo.

She didn't say anything else, though, and for a second I wondered what to do. I wouldn't normally be too keen on going a second round with an opponent who had just killed me. But it seemed like the despondent Darkness couldn't bring herself to ask to go back and fight the hydra again.

"…Things didn't work out today," I said after a second, "but the next time we fight that hydra, we'll make sure we have a plan. All right?"

"Wha—?!"

I couldn't help but tease her a little. "What, all that talk about keeping the citizens safe and stuff, and you were just gonna give up on that monster?"

"I was not, you idiot! Who do you think I am?! Protecting the populace is the very mission of the Dustiness family! The next time we meet that hydra, it's done for!"

Ah, the familiar bluster. I felt like I had gotten a little bit of the old Darkness back.

Having both taken our baths and gotten rid of the delightful smell, we arrived at the Adventurers Guild. I assumed Aqua and Megumin were already finished making the report. I opened the door, and…

"Why?! Why must you always do these outrageous things to us?!"

"It's true! Aqua, you remember the other day when you turned the fishmonger's tank to pure water and killed all the fish he got from the ocean?"

"B-but I thought I was doing them a favor! That fish tank was so small. I thought the least I could do was give them some nice clean water."

"What do we do?! We can't deal with a Kowloon Hydra on our own!"

"M-Mommy! I wanna go home!"

"Pass around those wanted posters! More posters! One for every adventurer in town!"

The Guild was in an absolute uproar. Adventurers and staff were shouting, and right there in the middle of it all, Aqua was standing and weeping.

"Oh! Kazuma, Darkness, thank goodness you're here!" Megumin said when she spotted us. "You have to do something about this!" She worked her way through the commotion to reach us.

"And what is 'this'?" I asked. "What's got everyone so upset? It looks like they're all angry at Aqua, but I thought we did pretty well this time."

"W-we did! And the hydra would have woken up eventually with or without us, so there's no reason everyone should be this upset…" Megumin, never keen on confrontation, shrank into herself. Darkness grabbed a passing guild girl.

"Hey, what's going on here? I know we failed to defeat the monster, but there's no call to make this much fuss about it. We didn't manage to kill the thing, but at least we bought some time until the royal knights arrive."

"Th-that's just it. Your timing couldn't be worse. It seems there was some kind of problem in the capital, and the knights don't have time to trouble themselves with the likes of us..."

Some kind of problem?!

"Spill it! What's going on?! Is the capital in trouble?! Is my adorable little sister in danger?!"

"L-little sister? No, it sounds like the trouble occurred a short while ago and is mostly over now. It seems nothing serious came of it. Right now, the knights are on a manhunt for this person who turned the capital upside down..."

I felt my heart start beating again. I had been on the verge of running off to the capital myself.

"Apparently, a group calling itself the Silver-Haired Thief Brigade actually managed to infiltrate the royal castle..."

Darkness and I both just about choked. The employee didn't seem to notice us, though. She held out a sheet of paper. "Just two people managed to overcome the royal knights and a group of highly capable adventurers to boldly rob the castle of several important treasures."

I took the paper and looked at it. It was a wanted poster. Across the top it read, SILVER-HAIRED THIEF BRIGADE. It depicted a villainous-looking guy in a mask, along with a silver-haired boy. The reward was two hundred million eris.

Man oh man. They were offering almost as much for me as for a general of the Demon King...

"Two hundred million... *Two hundred* million..."

"D-Darkness? Don't look at me like that."

Darkness normally showed no particular interest in money, but she was holding a wanted poster and giving me the crazy eye.

The Guild employee gave us a somewhat puzzled look but said, "The upshot is that we don't know when or if a unit of knights will actually come here."

Crap! That makes pretty much everything our fault.

The employee, totally oblivious to my mounting anxiety, continued, "But there is some hope. A few of the knights went all the way to Crimson Magic Village to see a famous fortune-teller who would tell them where the criminal was. Apparently, the fiend is right here in Axel! And the knights are on his trail like a pack of hounds!"

I broke out in a sweat.

"So we need your help, Mr. Kazuma Satou. You and your party have such good luck with big bounties like this one—if you can catch the thief, I'm sure the knights will be able to spare some men to help us!"

"Uhhh... I'm sure you're...right," I said. I was trying to act calm, but Darkness jabbed me with her elbow.

"It's only a matter of time until they catch the thief," she said. "After all, our own town is home to a fortune-teller even more powerful than the one in Crimson Magic Village!"

I knew who she meant. Someone wearing a mask very much like the one shown on this wanted poster.

This was bad. That demon loved his money, and for a bounty like mine, I was sure he would turn in his own business partner without so much as a second thought.

Suddenly, Darkness was frowning and trembling. The Guild employee clenched her fist as if to emphasize how high her expectations were.

"I just know you'll do everything you can to help us, Mr. Satou!"

She smiled widely.

I, of course, decided to go full shut-in.

5

"One day in the woods, there a mighty dragon stood..."

Aqua sat with her feet up on the sofa, looking out the window at the pouring rain as she hummed a song. As ever, she was holding her egg, projecting a beam of warm light onto it from her palm. She claimed that singing to the egg was a way of helping the animal inside learn before he was born.

Megumin jumped up and said, loudly enough to drown out Aqua's singing, "Kazuma, revenge! We must take revenge on that hydra!"

I was sitting cross-legged on the floor, brushing Chomusuke.

It had been three days since we'd fled the Adventurers Guild. Now that I knew people were on the hunt for me personally, I stuck close to Aqua to avoid Vanir's future vision and never left the house.

The miserly demon seemed to have trouble seeing people who were around Aqua; it was my good luck that Aqua, still obsessed with hatching her egg, never left the house, either.

Megumin, apparently impatient with the shut-in lifestyle, urged us on a daily basis to seek revenge.

"I heard you before," I said, "but how exactly are we supposed to defeat that monster? I've been thinking about it, but I haven't been able to come up with a good plan."

Megumin clutched her staff and clenched her teeth. "Firepower is the answer! We need to hit it with even more! If one Explosion isn't enough, we must drop them on the foe until it is wiped out of existence! If you could use Drain Touch to transfer Aqua's MP to me like you did during the battle with Mobile Fortress Destroyer, I believe it would be possible!"

Megumin's impassioned argument caused Aqua to leave off singing. "No way. Why should I have to be subject to some corrupt Lich skill like Drain Touch? I'm tired of having to put up with that. Kazuma can try to threaten me and Darkness can try to bribe me and you can go as crazy as you like, Megumin, but I say no way. My holy MP isn't something I dole out to just anyone!"

I gently ran the brush along Chomusuke's tail. "And what have you been doing with your oh-so-important MP lately? You don't have to look after that egg every waking minute. Just leave it in front of the fire. If you leave it too long, you can just have it for lunch."

"You're gonna get a taste of my holy *fist* the next time you mention snacking on this egg. I'll have you know that I'm pouring MP into this dragon egg. Dragons can practically be described as balls of magic, so the more MP they have, the stronger they are. And *this* dragon is going to stand above all his kinfolk! As his mother, I want to do everything I can for him."

...She was bent on insisting she had a dragon egg. Fine. Forget about her.

"Anyway, Megumin, why do you want revenge so badly? I know Darkness has some weird fixation on this hydra, but what have you got against it?"

"Well, you know, this and that. For starters, it did kill you. Should I not want to avenge you with my own hands?"

"O-oh. Gosh. Well, that's..."

I had to admit, hearing that had a certain appeal.

"Recently, Darkness and I have been going to the hydra's lake every day, using Darkness's Decoy skill to draw it out, and then hitting it with Explosion before fleeing home. But despite our persistent harassment, we can't figure out any other good way of dealing with it."

"I *thought* I hadn't heard the daily *boom* outside recently. So that's what you've been up to! Right now the monster doesn't seem too interested in attacking the town or anything, so don't antagonize it. And you, Darkness! You've been encouraging her? I thought it was your job to stop her from doing stuff like that!"

"Er, hmm," Darkness muttered from where she was seated on the carpet, polishing her armor. She couldn't bring herself to look at me. "But I so desperately want to defeat that hydra. And this is a way of whittling down its MP..."

It was obvious by now that she really did want to bring down the hydra herself. Not that I had any way of knowing why...

"Whatever. We can't do anything until this rain lets up anyway. We're talking about a water monster; trying to fight it in a downpour would only give it the advantage. When the rain stops, then we'll see what we can do."

Honestly, what I really wanted was to wait until the whole bounty-poster thing blew over.

"But it's the rainy season," Megumin said. "According to the weather fortune-teller, the rain won't stop for a while."

"When the rain lets up, we'll see what we can do."

"Why, you! What you're really saying is that you can't be bothered!"

"Hey, what're you doing? Stop it! Don't take it out on Chomusuke!"

Megumin had grabbed the brush and was trying to keep me from grooming Chomusuke's tail.

Out of all of us, only Darkness looked really serious as she sat there relentlessly polishing her armor.

6

Several days passed, but the rain didn't stop. Aqua and I stayed shut up in the house, while Darkness and Megumin kept going out to face the hydra.

Today was no different…

"We're home! I am sorry, but please prepare a bath. You know how Darkness is!"

In they came, Darkness carrying Megumin on her back and smelling sour.

"Did you get eaten *again*? I thought you were just going to smack it with an Explosion and run away. This is dangerous. You guys have to stop."

Darkness sloughed the immobile Megumin off onto the carpet, then started to remove her own armor, breathing heavily. She had just polished the stuff the other day, and now it was covered in scratches and spatters of hydra blood.

"That accursed beast!" she said. "Maybe it's not just chance that it's survived so many days of Explosions. Before I could use my Decoy skill, it ambushed us. Megumin didn't have time to chant her magic. That was a real tight spot... But we got out of it somehow, then I had Megumin hit it with Explosion, and while it was busy regenerating its heads, we got away. I guess beating this thing really isn't as simple as it seems."

She sighed, even as Aqua wandered up and cast Heal on her. When Darkness finally had her armor off, she thanked Aqua and then headed for the bath.

"...Hey, Kazuma," Aqua said, "can you really not think of any ideas of how to score a quick victory over that hydra? You're so weak, but your redeeming features are your wide range of not very valuable skills and the way you can think of a dirty trick to get out of any situation."

"Oh, hey, something just came to me. First we tie you up in chains, and then we throw you into the lake. When the hydra swallows you, we get a whole bunch of adventurers to pull on the chains and fish it up. Then we make sure it can't get back in the water and beat the stuffing out of it. What do you think?"

"""......"""

Aqua launched herself at me, but I grabbed her egg and held it hostage until she calmed down.

"Personally," Megumin said, "I don't have any problem with it, given that I can make use of my Explosion. But don't you think Darkness has been acting a bit strange lately?"

She looked in the direction of the bath, where Darkness had retreated.

"...Phew. ...? Uh, Kazuma, what are you doing to my armor?"

When Darkness came back from her bath, she found me crouched next to her armor. Megumin was sitting beside me, watching me work.

"I'm fixing it. It was all beat up when you came home today. You know how rainy it's been recently. I've been looking for stuff I can do here at home." I worked out the dents in the armor with a mallet, using my Smith skill for the first time in a while.

Darkness almost seemed to turn shy. "You know, I remember you fixing my armor on the road when we went to the hot springs together, too." She paused. "I'd like it if we could all go back there again."

"Not me," I said. "I can't stand that town. Those people are nuttier than Megumin."

"Hey! I shall have you tell me what kind of nuts we are talking about!"

I shoved her away—I was trying to work, here—as Darkness looked on in amusement.

"Yeah, but…even so, I wouldn't mind," she murmured. Her words seemed to carry a deeper meaning.

Some time later…

"Kazuma, she's not here! When I went to wake her up, her room was empty!"

"Ohhh, that Crusader! I explicitly told her not to go to that lake anymore. Why must she be such a terrible listener?!"

Darkness, who had told Megumin it was too dangerous to bring along any companions, had started going to the hydra's lair on her own each day. She ignored our attempts to stop her and would come home ragged every time. We started taking turns guarding her, but…

"How could you be asleep, you idioooot?!"

"Waaaaah! I'm tired, too, you know! I take care of Emperor Zel all day! Being a parent is hard work! You could stand to have a little sympathy!"

"Parent, my ass! Gimme that egg! I'm starting to think it looks mighty tasty!"

"Stop! I've been heating that egg for so long that if you broke it open now, something terrible might happen! If you saw what was inside, it would break your heart!"

Aqua clutched the egg to her stomach and hunched over so she looked like a turtle. I was practically spitting as I bellowed, "Who cares about a stupid egg right now anyway?! Darkness is more important! What the hell does she think she's doing?! Is it some stupid thing about a Crusader's duty or her mission as a noble to protect this town or whatever?"

"We can worry about Darkness's motivation later," Megumin said. "That hydra is learning. Darkness gets hurt worse and worse every day—we can't let this go on forever!" Never a fan of unexpected situations, she was clutching her staff.

I estimated that Darkness had snuck out of the house around dawn.

"Hey, Kazuma, is there really nothing we can do about that hydra? I'm going to drop off my egg at Wiz's shop, then Megumin and I are going to chase down Darkness and give her a piece of our minds. Do you want to come along? Although I'll understand if you're too scared to face an enemy who's already killed you once."

She was still crouched over her egg. It was an unusual thing to hear from Aqua, who typically wasn't much into conflict and battles.

If even she was up to doing this, then I could hardly stay at home by myself…

Ahh, dammit!

"There's somewhere I need to go. You two, just bring Darkness home somehow. If you run into the hydra, *don't* fight it. Just run back here."

The two girls nodded.

Left alone in the house, I grabbed some eris bills from my room and put them nonchalantly into my wallet.

"That stupid idiot. I guess I've got no choice!"

To help my stubborn noblewoman, I would do what I had to do.

7

The next morning.

I got up early and headed for the lake.

On their way to the lake the day before, Aqua and Megumin had run into a battered and dirty Darkness heading in the opposite direction. Darkness told me later, with an embarrassed smile, that Aqua had healed her wounds and then lectured her all the way home.

It looked like our Crusader genuinely had no intention of leaving the hydra alone.

I looked at the lake that spread out before me, waiting for Darkness. I was sure she would come, and I presumed Aqua and Megumin would be with her.

Finally, around noon, Darkness showed up with our other companions in tow. She stopped short, and her mouth hung open when she saw us.

That's right, *us*: Standing behind me was every adventurer I could find in Axel Town.

As Darkness stood immobile, the gathered adventurers began to call out to her:

"Hey! You're late, Lalatina!"

"I knew you'd come, sweet Lalatina!"

"Lalatina!"

"Lalatina!!"

"..."

"Stop it, Lalatina! They only called you by your name—you need to stop silently strangling me! St-stop! Quit it already!"

The teasing of the adventurers had caused Lalatina to grab me, weeping.

"What's the big idea, Kazuma? If this is some new form of harassment, two can play that game!"

"No! Why would I get all these people together for something as dumb as that? I just told everyone that you'd been fighting the Kowloon Hydra all by yourself day after day and begged them for help!"

"—?!"

Darkness let go of my shirt and looked around at everyone gathered there.

"Look! Lalatina's turning red!"

"Be nice! I know what she looks like, but our dear Lalatina is still a delicate young woman. We need sweet Lalatina's strength to defeat the hydra. What'll we do if you make her run home crying?"

"And Kazuma's been good about keeping us all in wine. Yesterday he treated us to some of the most expensive stuff available! Nothing wrong with doing him a good turn. Whatever Lalatina wants, Lalatina gets!"

"You hear that, Darkness?" I interjected. "Look at all the people who came out to help when they heard about the stupid things you were doing every day, stupid. It's one thing to have muscles for brains, but you've got to stop worrying people like this."

Darkness, blushing furiously, replied in a small voice, "Th-thanks…"

"I'm sorry? What's that?"

I was hoping to force her to repeat it much more loudly, but she only glared at me with teary eyes and looked around again, still embarrassed, at everyone there. Each time someone met her eyes, they looked away bashfully again or gave a friendly smile. After a minute, Darkness herself started to smile, too.

"Everyone, thank y—"

"Waaaaah! Kazuma! Kazuma!! I'm not sure, but I think the hydra is waking up faster than usual!"

The interruption came from Aqua, who had gone into the lake at some point.

At the same time, Megumin, preparing her magic on the shore, said, "That's why I told you it would be better not to get in the lake until Kazuma's signal!"

"But! But!! I wanna get home so I can see Zel hatch…!"

Aqua's timing couldn't have been worse for Darkness, who had finally mustered the courage to thank everyone. Now the Crusader stood blushing and quivering.

There was a massive splash as the Kowloon Hydra launched itself out of the water after Aqua.

"Each and every one of you is completely, utterly useless!"

Battle, start!

8

Things began a little more suddenly than I would've liked, but basically the battle went like this:

"Thieves, you have your steel wires? Archers, get your hook-tipped arrows ready and wait for my signal!"

"Waaaaaah, do it! Do it fast!"

Step one: Aqua lures the hydra to the water's edge.

"Tanks, hold position—it's your job to make sure the back row stays safe!"

Step two: Men and women in armor ward off the hydra's attacks.

"Wizards, get those spells ready to use at any time! I'm looking for the most powerful stuff you've got! Put everything into it; we're not going to get a second try!"

"Just leave it to me! This time my Explosion shall definitively decimate that deplorable dastard!"

Step three: We get our biggest, baddest magic ready to strike the finishing blow.

And then…

"Darkness, you get right in front of that thing and use your Decoy skill! This is all down to your toughness! Don't let it make mincemeat of you this time!"

"Who do you think I am?! Everything else aside, defense is the one thing no one can best me at!"

Step four: Darkness gets the hydra's attention and fights it head-on!

"Hey, Kazuma! What about me? What should I be doing?"

"If you've already buffed everybody, then there's nothing for you to do until people start getting hurt! Just pick somewhere out of the way and cheer us on!"

"Aww, no fair! I want something to do, too!"

And then, when Darkness had the hydra pinned down…

"Darkness! You're up!"

"Damn right I am! Hey! I'm the one you want! *Decoy*!"

Darkness activated her skill from her place on the lakeshore. While the hydra was distracted, I used my Ambush skill to make myself as inconspicuous as possible as I crept toward the monster.

Those eight heads could have sent any of the rest of us straight to Eris, as I already knew from experience. Darkness, however, just set her jaw and endured the full force of the monster's attack.

"""""*Bind*!"""""

The hydra came up on land to pursue Darkness, and the moment its eight heads were all in roughly the same place, the thieves used their wires to tie the creature's various necks together. At the same moment, the archers let loose with their hooked arrows. The arrows would have bounced off the creature's hard scales, but they lodged themselves nicely among the wires.

Once the adventurers were confident the hooks were set, they began a great tug-of-war on the attached ropes. This brought the hydra even farther away from the lake and prevented it from running away.

As all this was happening, I was getting close with Ambush until I jumped on the hydra's back, feeling its scales under my hands.

"If you have to be out of MP before we can kill you, then let me help you get rid of all that magic!"

The instant I started using Drain Touch to absorb its MP, the hydra started thrashing wildly. I guess Aqua did say something about dragons being basically living lumps of magical power—this critter was awfully sensitive to having its magic absorbed.

"Yippee ki-yay! It's working! It's— Whoaaaaa!"

When I started draining its magic, the hydra began fighting furiously to free its necks, but restrained by Bind, it couldn't reach me on its back.

One of the adventurers watching the scene cried out, "Kazuma, get out of there! What are you, nuts?! What do you think you're doing up there?"

"It's okay! I'm using one of my secret skills to help weaken this big lug! Wizards, when all its MP is gone, let loose with your—"

That was as far as I got before the hydra twisted its whole body and tried to slam its back into the ground.

Crud!

"Eeeyiiikes! I'm gonna get smooshed!"

"Idiot! What do you think you're doing?!" As I was thrown from the hydra's back, Darkness immediately covered me with her body. Notwithstanding the fact that I had been nearly crushed, having Darkness that close to me got me in a bit of a tizzy. As the hydra came rolling over, Darkness put herself in a push-up position to prevent me from being squished.

"That's my Miss Dustiness! Endurance and upper body strength till the cows come home!"

"Shut your mouth and move your butt! I can't…go on like this…"

Darkness may or may not have been fine if the hydra continued to roll over on us, but for me, it definitely wouldn't have been pretty.

With Darkness red-faced above me, I reached out toward the hydra. "Keep going, Darkness!" I said. "You have to hold out a little longer; don't give up! Just stay right where you are!"

"I-is this—? Is this the fabled edging play?! I'm sorry, I can't—it's too much…!"

Darkness had been here every day, whittling away the hydra's MP. I wasn't about to let all her effort go to waste by letting this thing get away now!

I simultaneously threw myself into two separate activities: using Drain Touch and scolding Darkness.

"You finally decide to start being some help and you're already finished?! I thought you were planning to defend your title in the Endurance Championship! And you can't even put up with this? Finish what you started! Are you really gonna give up so easily with all these adventurers watching?!"

"—?! Being physically crushed by a hydra and emotionally crushed by this man's words at the same time! What have I done to deserve such a reward?! Why today of all days?!"

Darkness's whole body was shaking, her face red and her eyes brimming with tears. Every muscle was dripping with sweat, but somehow she managed to hold out.

I continued to drain the monster with all my might. The hydra flung its captive heads around, slamming them into Darkness.

"Pull! Puuull!" The beefy adventurers who had been guarding our back row were now pulling mightily on the ropes attached to the arrows attached to the wires attached to the hydra. Apparently, they intended to rescue Darkness from her trial of endurance.

Darkness gave me a contented smile and whispered, "I… I can't hold on anymore… But d-don't…worry, Kazuma… At least we'll die together…"

"Oh, I'm worried! Don't you quit! I'm the only one who would die anyway! You're the one with all the buffs and everything! You think just being squashed flat by a hydra would kill you?!"

My equipment at that moment was minimal, partly because most of my gear had been dissolved in the hydra's stomach the other day. At this rate, with my laughably weak defenses, I was as good as dead.

And I was *not* keen on dying twice in such a short time.

"If—if I give up, you'll die… Ahh! What is this? You're ordering me to endure, almost as if you were my master, and yet at the same time, I hold your life in my hands! Oh, the paradox! Which of us is the master now?! I've never tasted such a sensation before, Kazuma…!"

Great. What had happened to the thoughtful, serious Darkness I'd seen recently? The cool one?

It was at that moment of utmost crisis that we heard it:

"Look! The hydra's weak now! And it can't even move! I lay claim to the great bounty, the Kowloon Hydra! The money goes to whoever kills it—all the money! I'm not sharing with anyone!"

"Hold on, how can you say that in a situation like this?! And it *can* move—it's just that its heads are bound. So watch out! Oh! Dust! Duuust!"

I recognized those voices. At the same moment, the weight on top of us lightened considerably. Some strong, brave person must have pulled the hydra off us at last.

Darkness and I managed to crawl out from under the rampaging monster and scuttle back to where Megumin was waiting.

"*Light of Saber*!!"

I knew that spell from all the times I had heard it invoked at Crimson Magic Village. I looked in the direction of the voice to discover that Yunyun of the Crimson Magic Clan had inserted herself into the battle at some point and launched her spell at the hydra's heads. It looked like someone had been eaten and she was rescuing them.

Actually, why hadn't I noticed her there sooner? Was she just that easy to miss? Come to think of it, I remembered somebody hesitantly calling out to me on the way here, but I had been so busy thinking about Darkness…

Then one of the adventurers shouted, "Check it out! The head she cut off isn't regenerating!"

I looked for myself, and sure enough, the hydra was down to seven heads. It looked like the monster was trying to flee back into the lake, but several heavily armored adventurers tugged on the ropes and made sure it stayed where it was.

"Okay, wizards, you're up!"

I shouted to our magic users, who had been waiting eagerly to unleash all of their most powerful spells.

"Open fire!"

At my order, a storm of magic slammed into the hydra. Fireballs and lightning bolts went flying, including the full wrath of two Crimson Magic Clan mages.

"*Light of Saber*!!!" A blindingly bright blade of light sliced at the hydra's necks as Yunyun gave Megumin a triumphant look.

A corner of Megumin's mouth twitched upward; her red eyes flashed, and she brandished her staff.

“Explosion magic incoming!” shouted someone, no doubt from Axel Town and of long acquaintance with Megumin’s magic. “Everyone near the water’s edge, evacuate!”

“Cover your ears!” someone else yelled.

“Now! Now I shall take revenge for Kazuma! May this be a flower I offer at his grave, a fragrant blossom whose aroma he can smell up in heaven…!”

Hey. Revenge is all well and good, but I’m standing right here.

“*Explosion*!!!!”

The light from Megumin’s staff lanced toward the hydra, which had already been the subject of so much magical abuse. The bounty head that had made this area a wasteland for so long gave one last, great scream before it went to its eternal rest.

9

“You must recognize my victory! I eliminated six hydra heads, whereas you were responsible for only two, Yunyun! Anyone can see which of these numbers is greater!”

“Wh-why should you win, Megumin? You just stood around until the hydra was nearly unconscious! I was out there helping to rescue someone who got eaten; I must get points for that!”

“Yes, perhaps *one* point, for rescuing a punk who thought he was going to claim the entire reward for himself and instead only got swallowed. But if you truly consider yourself a member of the Crimson Magic Clan, then surely you understand the importance of waiting for the right moment to grab your glory!”

With the hydra in the books, we and the other adventurers were going back to Axel in high spirits. Megumin and Yunyun (the former having strong-armed the latter into giving her a piggyback ride) had been going at it like this all the way home.

Despite how powerful our opponent had been, we had finished the job with just a single casualty, and that person had already been resurrected by Aqua.

Keith and Rin, whose party I had once joined, were chatting with me.

"Man, oh man," Keith was saying. "I guess we really can do great things when we need to! Er, although maybe it wouldn't have been possible without you and your party, Kazuma."

"That's for sure," Rin said. "I know we agreed to split the bounty, but you guys should definitely get more. Maybe you can take the share of the idiot who said that the one who kills the hydra gets all the money."

The truth was, though, that it had taken all of us to bring down this monster. And so…

"All right, then!" I said. "I know we're all tired from that hydra. Let's take it easy today and get our reward tomorrow!"

"""""Yeah! Whoo-hoo!"""""

"You've gotta be kiiiidding!"

I thought I heard a disappointed moan mixed in with the cheering. I glanced over happily at Darkness, who was walking beside me. The nervousness and unhappiness she had shown lately were gone, as if she had been freed of whatever had been possessing her.

"So how do you feel now that the hydra's gone? Think you can start getting some sleep again?"

"I do. You've helped me figure out a few different things," she said. "Things I now feel silly for having worried so much about. But it's not the death of the hydra that's made me feel better." She smiled for the first time in days. "I remembered how much I like the people in this town. That's helped me get over my hesitation. I'm not afraid anymore, and I won't have any regrets."

"Every once in a while, you manage to keep a straight face saying something that would embarrass anyone else."

Darkness pinched my side gently in response to my teasing. Then she said:

* * *

"I can't tell you how happy I am."

Again, someone else might feel silly making a declaration like that.

"Hey, venerate me more! Praise me! Say, 'Thank you so much for so generously bringing me back to life, Lady Aqua!'"

"Yo, Kazuma! It's great to be back from the dead and all, but this priest of yours is really getting on my nerves!"

Chapter 3
May I Lecture This Runaway Girl!

1

"All adventurers who participated in yesterday's battle—your work is very, very, very much appreciated! Our heartfelt congratulations on your defeat of the giant bounty head, the Kowloon Hydra! In light of your actions, you'll all receive a huge reward!"

""""""Whooooooooooooo!!""""""

The Guild employee's announcement prompted the adventurers present to fill the Guild Hall with cheers.

With the hydra safely dead, we had all gone home to rest from the massive battle before reconvening here at the Guild. All in attendance had been at the previous day's fight, and they all looked very happy. That made sense, given the reward they were about to receive.

My party was camped out at a table in the center of the hall. "I don't get it," I said. "We're gonna pick up a huge sack of cash, and Darkness isn't even here. Did she forget we were having a party today? Or is she embarrassed about that stuff yesterday?"

"That might be it," Aqua said. "I felt like there was a little more… tension than usual with Darkness yesterday. Like maybe she was embarrassed even around us. She hardly ever drinks, but yesterday she really hit the bottle. She even tried to get me to drink, even though she usually yells at me when she thinks I've had too much wine."

Aqua was holding her egg in her hand, which, as ever, gave off a faint glow. She seemed to be trying to act grown-up as she said, "Darkness is the oldest person in our party, but she can be so childish, you know? She's clumsy and quick to be embarrassed. If she doesn't feel she can show her face around here yet, there's nothing we can do about it. Best just let her watch after the house. Maybe we can bring her a souvenir."

"How can you act like she's the oldest *and* the youngest member of our party at the same time? Anyway, which of you is the lady who's so old she won't even tell us how old she is?"

"Mr. Kazuma Satou. Didn't I warn you that the next time you brought up that subject, you were going to get some serious divine punishment? I hereby declare: May all your cold beverages be lukewarm!"

I didn't know how she could say such stupid things with a straight face, but I mostly ignored Aqua. Instead, I looked around at the adventurers gleefully awaiting their reward. The bounty was a billion eris, to be split among all those who had participated.

A billion eris.

That sum represented what they felt the defeat of the hydra was worth. With the monster gone, the area around the lake would become fertile again; the money was proportionate to the benefit of having rich new soil to farm.

Approximately fifty people had been part of this latest monster-slaying expedition. That meant twenty million eris each.

They called the adventurers up by name, one by one, until finally it was our turn.

"Mr. Kazuma Satou and party! In addition to the reward of eighty million eris, representing four shares, by special request of those who participated in the battle, you are also to be awarded one extra share, for a total of one hundred million eris!"

"Thank you so much! All right, everyone! Let's put this extra twenty million to good use right here and— H-hey! Leggo! You didn't want to hand over the last bag of money, either!"

I had to pry the cash out of the unwilling hand of the Guild employee.

"Thanks again for your help yesterday, everyone! Now let's party!"

"""""""Whoooooooooooooo!!!"""""""

The whooping and hollering filled the entire Guild Hall.

It was only noon, but I foresaw myself having a late night…

2

It was well after sunset as we walked through the streets of Axel, making our way back to the mansion.

With the hydra defeated, for once we hadn't a care in the world, and we had bought some stuff a cut above what we usually got. I thought we could use it to have ourselves a little after-party with Darkness at home.

What did we get? Speckled crab! I hadn't had it since Darkness's family had sent us some as a gift. Aqua had been exceptionally excited ever since she saw it.

When we got back, though, Darkness was nowhere to be found.

"Hey, Darkness, we're…home? Huh? What, did she go out?"

Then I noticed a single sheet of paper on the table. It was a note in Darkness's handwriting, and it said she had gone to the local lord to report the slaying of the hydra. (The mansion of the local ruler, which I had destroyed some time ago, had finally been rebuilt.)

Now that we were back home, Aqua took her egg out of her pocket, sat on the couch, and got back to the business of trying to hatch it, but not without urging me to hurry up with the food, like a puppy waiting for her dinner.

"Hey, pipe down," I said. "We have to wait till Darkness gets home before we can eat anyway. And another thing. Stop trying to hatch your dumb chick for a few minutes and help out around the house a little! Have you been cleaning the bathroom like you're supposed to?"

"Hey, Kazuma, you could afford to be a little nicer to a woman who's practically on the verge of childbirth. And I want you to stop calling him a chick already. You're so mean to Emperor Zel, and he hasn't even been born yet—when he gets big, don't be surprised if he eats you."

Finally, Megumin and I decided to make dinner on the assumption that Darkness would be home sooner or later. The remaining member of our party was too busy hatching an egg to help, so she just lazed around on the sofa.

At last our nicer-than-usual meal was ready and laid out on the living room table.

"Hey, Kazuma, Darkness is pretty late. I don't think I can hold out with the food sitting in front of me like this. Hurry up and find Darkness! Go find her!"

"You're awfully demanding for someone who didn't pay for the food or help make it," I replied.

Meanwhile, Megumin got silverware and tea for four. "This is a rather special meal. Even a daughter of nobility like Darkness doesn't get speckled crab very often, I should think. Heh-heh-heh! I look forward to seeing her reaction when she tastes my cooking!"

"You just shook some salt over it and then got the silverware."

I couldn't blame Megumin, though, for seeming pleased. We were eating well tonight, if I did say so myself. I had started to acquire refined tastes from constantly going out to eat, so finally I had shelled out some money to learn the Cook skill.

After all, from here on out, I intended to engage in adventuring only as a hobby. That meant skills that would improve my quality of life were worth more to me than combat abilities. Maybe I could take some of my loads of money and open a restaurant or something…

I mulled over the idea as all of us waited eagerly for Darkness to come home.

Finally, the curtain of night had well and truly fallen, and Darkness still hadn't come home.

"Hey, Kazuma! The food's gone all cold! Heat it up again!"

"Forcing someone to wait for their food… I'm not Darkness, and I do not enjoy this kind of 'play' at all. As punishment, when she gets home, I shall make her sit in front of the sofa and watch while we eat first."

"I don't think she would find that as punishing as you hope. In fact, I think she might… Er, forget it. She really is pretty late, though. She said she'd be back by dinner. What is she up to? Maybe something happened at her home, just like Vanir predicted? She could at least send us a message or something."

None of us was very happy to be waiting. At length, irritation turned to anger, and we convened an impromptu conference about how we would get back at her for this. It was a surprisingly thorny question, given that she took most punishments as more like rewards. What would work on someone like that?

The only thing none of us suggested was that we go ahead and eat.

We settled on forcing her to wear an absolutely adorable outfit (coordinated by Aqua) and then parading her through the Guild and town, taking photos with a magical camera, despite the fact that such equipment would be very expensive to rent for even a day.

By the time we had figured out what we were going to do to Darkness, today was about to turn into tomorrow.

"Boy, she's really late," Aqua murmured. And still no one touched their food.

How could it take this long to report the defeat of one hydra? I knew the guy she was reporting it to was a famous lecher, but I didn't think even he would try anything with Darkness, who was nobility, after all.

It looked like she wouldn't be coming home today, no matter how long we waited. That meant she'd be getting back in the morning again, and then we would really let her have it.

"I don't think she's coming back today," I said. "I wish she'd at least let us know. Hey, let's just eat already."

But despite my suggestion, Aqua and Megumin didn't budge. They just sat there looking disturbed.

Ahh, dammit!

I'm gonna make that big, dumb masochist cry for real. Maybe I can rent Vanir for an hour and have him ask her every embarrassing question he can come up with.

Okay, I've got it. The longer she takes to come home, the longer I'll let Vanir interrogate her.

Now I had a plan. But Darkness didn't come home that day. Or the next day. Or even the one after that.

For days on end, she didn't come home at all.

3

"Hey, Kazuma, what's that? What are you making?"

I was at the living room table, where I had been working industriously all morning. Aqua picked up the product of my labors and inspected it.

It was basically imitation dynamite. It was back-to-basics stuff, like the kind Nobel had first made: nitroglycerin mixed with sand and a hardening agent, wrapped in paper and topped with a fuse.

But then, nitroglycerin hadn't yet been discovered in this world, and I couldn't find anything that would make for a good fuse, so even if you lit this thing on fire, it wouldn't explode. I didn't actually know how dynamite worked, so I couldn't exactly build some for myself…

"It's… You know. I have kind of this vague idea of the shape and what's involved, but we don't have the right materials, so I can't make the real thing. But I thought if I could make something with the right shape, maybe some visionary would be able to find something to use in place of nitro."

"I see! You're bringing hypermodern weapon technology into a world that knows nothing of it! Kazuma… You terrify me…!"

Actually, it was more like I'd decided to go ahead and revisit a few ideas I had previously rejected on the grounds that no one would want them. But who knew? Maybe they'd sell.

Aqua held her egg to her stomach with one hand and picked up the dynamite in the other.

There was a reason I was doing this.

Early this morning, a letter had arrived from Darkness.

"That thing that Aqua is holding, what are you going to use it for?" Megumin looked up from her intent perusal of Darkness's letter.

"This is a replica of something called dynamite. Dynamite basically has the same effect as explosion magic."

"?!"

Megumin grabbed the item out of Aqua's hand. My words seemed to have provoked a pretty serious reaction.

"Dynamite is great, because anyone can use it," I went on. "It's so simple, it doesn't even need MP! We still have a ways to go, but as far as making it—"

"Grrrarraaahhh!"

"Ahhhhhh! How can you do that to something I worked so hard on?!"

Megumin had run over to the window and flung the dynamite out with all her might.

"Shall I abide the 'simple' reproduction of the ultimate magic?! I will not allow the development of such evil weapons!"

"Y-you're such a pain…"

Megumin stood with rasping breath for a moment before she remembered the letter.

It had come from Darkness, addressed to all of us. Megumin had read it over more times than I could count, sure there must be some hidden meaning. Now she placed it on the table.

"Darkness really intends to leave our party… To never come back…"

Aqua and I were both silent at that.

Finally, I said, "…There's nothing any of us can do. Family is family. She should never have been able to go adventuring with commoners like us in the first place."

"No! I'm sure there's something strange going on here," Megumin shot back. "Darkness would never just leave us without saying anything! We're too close for her to say farewell with nothing but a letter!"

"She's right," Aqua said. "You know what I think? I think Kazuma's over-the-top sexual harassment finally went too far. At the very least, he could stop filling the bathtub with our laundry and then diving in while crying, 'Whoo-hoo! Underwear baaaath!'"

"What?! I have never once done that! Yet!"

"'Yet'?"

I grabbed the letter off the table and reviewed the contents once again.

I'm sorry for springing this on you so suddenly.

As I read it over...

I can't tell you exactly what's going on, but it's complicated. It's something I have to deal with as a noble.

...I crushed it into a ball and prepared to throw it into the trash bin.

I can't be with you guys anymore. I know how selfish it sounds, but count me out of the party. I hope you'll find another fine frontline defender.

Seeing me like that, Aqua and Megumin looked a little scared. Dammit, what was I so angry about?

I'm grateful to all of you. I can never express just how thankful I am. I truly enjoyed our adventures together. This has been the best time of my life. I promise I'll never forget the experiences we shared together.

She was nobility, after all. She lived in a different world than we did. She'd just gone back to it.

Yeah... Yeah. Now we could get a real tank, someone whose attacks actually landed. That was the plan.

I sat down at the table and started on my next product.

Thank you for everything. Signed, Lalatina Ford Dustiness. To my beloved companions, I express my gratitude from the bottom of my heart.

There was a crack as the tip of my box cutter broke. I had been pushing harder with it than I'd realized. That caused Megumin to say, "I believe you are bothered as well, aren't you, Kazuma? Why not be honest? And then let us go once more to Darkness's mansion!"

She clenched her fist in determination and came closer to me.

That first day Darkness hadn't come home—

Shortly after midnight, we started picking at the cold food.

Then, straightaway that morning, we pretty much mounted an assault on the Dustiness mansion…

"They'll just chase us off again," I said. "We *are* talking about a serious noble family here. If we try to fight our way in, the best we can hope for is that we all get arrested. Darkness and her dad being who they are, we might avoid the death penalty, but if she doesn't want to see us, we don't have a lot of choices."

Megumin wilted at this.

When we had arrived at Darkness's home, the guard at the gate had told us simply, "I can't tell you what's happening. I must ask you to withdraw," and then turned us away.

Irritated, I started looking for a replacement box cutter.

"I don't think you believe what you're saying, Kazuma," Aqua said. "You're still hoping there's something we can do for Darkness. That's why you're working so hard on all this new stuff. You really believe what that useless demon said to you, don't you? Let me tell you something about demons. They're all con artists. And they never help someone for free."

I froze when I heard Aqua give voice to my inner turmoil. "N-no way! You're so wrong you don't even know! I just don't wanna work, so I'm coming up with even more gadgets to sell, that's all!"

Aqua looked at me very seriously. "What's with the passive-aggressive act, Kazuma? You don't have to pretend not to care. Just be honest. Say that you're lonely without Darkness around. I refuse to acknowledge anyone who tries that 'I pretend not to care, but I secretly care a lot!' act but doesn't have golden twintails! So either get your act together or get some dye and start doing that hair!"

"……"

I grabbed the egg from Aqua as if I was going to go make breakfast with it. That was enough to get her weeping and apologizing for crossing the line.

Megumin just watched us, then murmured sadly, "Even your usual antics are somehow…missing something now."

4

Megumin pattered behind me, looking displeased, as I went to the Guild. Frankly, I had hoped she would just sit quietly at home today—like Aqua, who was still obsessed with hatching her egg.

"Hey, Megumin," I said. "I'll give you some pocket change to blow—so just go home, okay?"

"No, it is not okay. I am a member of this party, and as such I have a right to help choose any new members."

Megumin had refused to listen to any of my instructions for a while now. And I guess I couldn't blame her.

After all, the reason I was going to the Guild right now was in hopes of finding a new frontline member to replace Darkness.

The wizard stepped up her pace until she was immediately behind me and said, "I'm appalled. A precious companion, with whom you've shared laughter and pain, goes away for just a few days, and you try to replace her? You're a monster, Kazuma. A true monster."

Then she jogged backward until she was again several steps behind me.

"Y-you've got it all wrong. Darkness *asked* us to replace her. Of course I would have preferred to have her back. But she's the one who wanted us to—"

There was a *tap-tap-tap* as Megumin closed the distance once more. "You're just putting up a front. You're embarrassed after what Aqua said to you earlier, aren't you? You just can't admit it. You're trying to act tough. You're afraid that if you put off getting a new party member, we'll think it's because you miss Darkness."

Then she jogged backward (*tap-tap-tap*) until she was again several steps behind me.

I can't believe this!

After that, Megumin tailed me until we got to the Guild, the space between us never changing by a single step.

Geez. She could just walk beside me, but nooo...

Annoyingly, she never fell back far enough that I could try to lose her by running away.

When we finally made it to the Adventurers Guild, Megumin came up and tugged on my sleeve.

"I really don't think you should go in there, Kazuma. If you do, you will experience firsthand the wrath of the Crimson Magic Clan."

"What are you gonna do? Try anything, and I'll stuff that precious staff of yours down the toilet."

I walked into the Guild with Megumin, who was frowning close behind me. I went over to the LOOKING FOR GROUP board and started going through the posts. There was no point in posting a request for new members myself; our party's terrible reputation would precede us. I was painfully aware that nobody would answer my request for a front-row tank.

That meant we had to find someone who was already looking for a new party to join. We could strong-arm them a little if necessary...

Ooh!

I actually found someone right away who looked pretty good. A warrior, specializing in one-handed swords. Confident in their defensive prowess, looking to tank on the front row. Eighteen-year-old male.

That sounded just about right. I grabbed the paper and went over to the table where the adventurer was waiting.

"Ahem. Excuse me? About your post?" I said.

The guy looked up at me with a cheerful expression. Maybe he didn't know who I was. "Oh yes! Pleased to meet you. My name is—"

"Never mind the introductions," Megumin said, coming up behind the guy.

...This couldn't end well.

"I don't want to know your name until I have tested you, to see if you are right for our party. We are, after all, a first-rate operation that routinely goes toe-to-toe with generals of the Demon King. Your test is this: You must defeat a major bounty solo, without any— Ow!"

"There's no test! Please, just ignore her! I'm sorry—give us a minute, okay?"

"Uh... Sure..."

I gave the jabbering Megumin a smack to shut her up. "Come over here, you."

"Absolutely not... Oh! Oh! Don't pull on my hood! I got this robe from a friend! You'll stretch it out of shape!"

I dragged Megumin over to where we would be out of earshot of the warrior guy. "Don't you get it?" I said. "If Darkness comes back, all that happens is we have a five-person party. I don't have the stamina to be our wall. Neither does Aqua. And you are out of the question. If we want to face a bunch of monsters without Darkness, we need someone to block for us, get it?"

"Yes, Kazuma, I 'get it.' I am quite intelligent enough to understand the need for front-row muscle. Let us proceed, then."

There's no way she really understands. She's going to sabotage the interview.

"Listen up," I said to her. "We've taken down a bunch of the Demon King's generals. One of these days we're going to get the attention of the king himself. Heck, he sent Vanir here because we offed Beldia. We need to have at least a minimum of functioning combat ability at any time, just in case he shows up. We could get that kid to join us on a temp basis. You see? You won't undermine me, will you?"

"I see. And I won't. Believe me, I won't." Megumin nodded, unusually docile. It was when she was most demure that you could be surest she was planning something. I went back to the warrior's table, keeping one very close eye on my wizard.

"Okay," I said, "sorry about that. I'm Kazuma Satou. You can call me Kazuma. And this is—"

Just as I was about to introduce her, Megumin gave her cape a dramatic flourish and, in a voice that carried around the entire Guild Hall, said:

"My name is Megumin! Greatest of the magic-users of Axel and master of Explosion! In this Guild I am known by the nickname of Crazy Explosion Girl! Now, let us together— Ow!"

As Megumin stood there doing a ridiculous self-introduction and attracting the attention of the entire Guild, I gave her a smack—but it was too late. A look of recognition was dawning on the warrior's face.

"W-wait... I've heard rumors about you... I'm—I'm sorry, they were the most terrible things. It's too much for me! Please, ask someone else!"

I was curious what kind of rumors he'd heard. Maybe our reputation was worse than I'd thought. We left the warrior, still apologizing, behind us. Megumin turned to me with a smile that was part satisfaction—but part pain, as if she had lost something important.

"It doesn't look like he's a good match for us, does it, Kazuma? All I did was introduce myself. Let's try the next person. Who is it?"

Self-introduction? More like a suicide attack. I had underestimated Megumin's commitment. I never expected her to embrace the nickname she loathed so much.

Anyway, who *was* next?

Megumin and I went back over to the board, but each time we found a likely prospect, they refused to so much as make eye contact.

It looked like Megumin had succeeded in fatally wounding our reputation with her little outburst.

Dammit! Usually she just mindlessly exploded things. Why did she have to choose now of all times to be clever?

That was when it happened.

"Hey, Kazuma. You lookin' for party members? Why not ask me?"

It was Dust. He didn't seem to be with his usual group today.

"You already have party members, don't you?" I said. "What happened to the others?"

Dust's face twisted. "They're the worst! Get this, Kazuma—just listen to this! They made all that money in the battle with the hydra, so now they tell me they don't plan to work for a while! I didn't get any reward, and I need to make some cash. But everyone's so loaded right now that they aren't even looking for temp party members. And warriors like me are an eris a dozen… That's my story. If you're looking to fill out your front row, why not let me do it?"

Megumin was glaring at Dust as if he were a very inconvenient bug. Okay, so he had a reputation as a punk, but he was also known as someone who could get a job done. Megumin and Aqua had actually partied up with him at one point, so he was sort of a friend.

I didn't have any reason to turn him down, so Dust joined our party on a trial basis.

What we needed now was a way to make sure the whole party gelled, temporary member and all, so we grabbed a random quest and headed for a big farming area on the outskirts of town.

It was the rainy season, and while in Japan that brings out cute little toads, around here it meant something much more dangerous.

"*Deadeye*! *Deadeye, Deadeye, Deadeye*! …This isn't working. I can't damage it with my arrows. Its skin is too tough!"

"Swords and arrows won't work against an Adamantropod! Just try to slow it down with magic, Kazuma! Help protect the fields from that thing until Little Miss Jailbait gets her magic ready!"

"Hey! Exactly whom do you think you're referring to as jailbait?!"

Dust, Megumin, and I were out in the fields along with several other adventurers who had taken the same quest to get rid of these pests. The rainy season brought a pestilence of Giant Snails, which liked to eat the crops—and then there were these Adamantropods.

Behind us, at that moment…

"Hey! One of those summer bamboos got Joseph right in the ass! He's wounded! He can't work in the fields like this! Get him out of here!"

"A wild boar! It must think all this confusion is its chance, because it and other crop eaters are showing up in droves!"

These shouts were coming from the farmers trying to harvest the crops.

Harvesting was a labor-intensive project in any world.

"*Freeze*! *Freeze, Freeze*! *Freeze*!!" I used ice magic to lower the Adamantropod's body temperature and slow it down. It didn't have the prefix *adamant-* in its name for nothing—not just its shell but its entire body was exceptionally tough. Buying us time like this was the most I could possibly do.

In the fields, Dust had already dispatched several monkeys and now stabbed another one with his sword, bracing himself with the hilt while he brought up the shield in his left hand.

A wild boar was about to charge, and Dust was getting ready to meet it.

"Come at meeeee!" Dust dropped into a low stance and ran forward, gripping the hilt of his sword even tighter. If anyone could face down a wild boar without flinching, it would be him. He had survived a violent attack by a hydra, after all.

But that would be a lot to expect, even from Dust. The boar, as big as a cow, went charging straight at him…

"Gwah?!"

The monster's attack flung him through the air. The pig, however, wasn't unscathed from its collision with Dust and his full suit of metal armor; it tottered around, dazed, and stopped charging. I went over to the boar and cut it down with my sword. I had managed to defeat the creature without actually having to fight it. I took a look back to see how things were going.

Monkeys had gotten past the defensive efforts of several adventurers and into the fields. *Damn!* I temporarily ignored Dust, still blinking from his encounter with the boar, and started sniping monkeys with my arrows.

"Kazuma! I have finished chanting my Explosion spell!" Megumin called.

I pointed at the retreating band of monkeys and said, "Do it, Megumin! Blow 'em away!"

That prompted shouting from the other adventurers: "No! Wai—"

"*Explosion*!!!"

Megumin's magic took out the monkeys, and the boar, and the Adamantropod. And all the fields, and all the crops, and all of us.

5

Threat eliminated, we headed back to the Guild. The reward was twenty thousand eris for each adventurer who participated. We were dealing with Adamantropods and some other pests—other than the wild boar, nothing life-threatening. Twenty thousand seemed like a pretty good deal…

For everyone else anyway.

"Right, then, Mr. Kazuma Satou, Miss Megumin, Mr. Dust. Five thousand eris each."

Blowing away the crops took a chunk out of our reward. That was on me; I had given Megumin the order without thinking it through.

I apologized, but Dust said to me, "Hey, it happens. At least this'll cover the booze for tonight. Don't get all bent out of shape. Without the big boom, those monkeys would've gotten away, and we would've failed the whole quest!"

Then he laughed and immediately put his money toward the order of a nice cold mug.

"You know," Megumin said, "given that neither Aqua nor Darkness was present, I think the three of us did quite well together. There weren't too many other adventurers, either. I would have expected more participants in that quest."

Megumin seemed happy enough that we had completed the quest successfully, but it still seemed like her mind was elsewhere. And I knew where: She was thinking about Darkness.

It wasn't fair to compare Dust with Darkness, but if there was one thing that crazy masochist was good at, it was soaking up damage. Dust had done himself proud, getting rid of some of the monkeys and being an all-around decent front-row fighter, but still... Darkness might never have hit anything with her attacks, but she could have absorbed that boar's charge without flinching. Again: not fair, I know, but I couldn't help thinking about it.

Well, what was the point of comparing Dust and Darkness now? Dust was the one we had in our party, and we would just have to see how things went.

The day after we had acquired this provisional party member, the front door of our house flew open without so much as a knock, and a man came dashing in.

"I know I said yesterday that, since you had joined our party for the time being, you should stop by the house and I would formally introduce you to Aqua—but you don't have to be in such a rush. What's up?"

The new arrival, Dust, was still breathing hard as he said, "Kazuma, this is bad! You gotta help me! I'm begging you—come with me!"

This was the guy who had charged right in to finish off a hydra.

Whatever had him this upset, it had to be big. I looked back at Megumin and Aqua. "I don't know what this is about, but I'm going to find out."

Then I left the mansion, Dust practically dragging me along.

As we went, Dust explained to me just what it was that was so terrible. When he finished, I suddenly stopped short.

"All right, hang on a minute. Let me get this straight. This awful situation you're so worried about...is that Rin got a guy?"

"Yes! Surely you can see how serious this is?! But all Keith and Taylor had to say was, *'Oh, huh'*!"

Sorry, buddy, that's...pretty much my reaction, too.

Dust, however, raised his fist and proclaimed, "My dear and treasured companion is getting all lovey-dovey with some dude from who knows where! Kazuma, wouldn't you be worried if one of your good female friends took up with some weird guy?!"

I guess if I, you know, had any good female friends... And if she went and got a boyfriend...

"I sort of get what you're saying. I think."

"Right?! That's my Kazuma; I knew you'd understand!"

Practically manic now, Dust went on with his story. From what he told me, Rin had grown colder and colder toward him recently. Suspicious, Dust had started tailing her twenty-four seven and had spotted her going to an inn with a guy he didn't recognize.

"Y-y'know, you really need to stop with the—"

"And that means this no-account rando has turned Rin into his arm candy! I'm worried about my dear party member. I want to find out who this guy is. Please, Kazuma, I can't count on the others. You're the only one I can trust—please help me!" He put his palms together in supplication.

I stopped and thought. It wasn't cool to interfere in other people's love lives, but could I really pretend I didn't know how he felt? If Darkness suddenly announced one day that she had a boyfriend, I would want to know who he was. Though, granted, that was because Darkness had…strange taste in guys.

"All right," I said after a moment. "I don't quite feel right about it, but if I were in your place, I might want the same thing. I don't think Rin is likely to get herself into any trouble, but we did go on an adventure together once. I'd be lying if I said I didn't want to know what kind of guy she's involved with."

"Yeah! I knew I could tell you, Kazuma! I knew I could count on you!"

I resumed walking down the street, slightly worried about Dust. In my mind, Rin overlapped with Darkness. I hadn't heard from her in so long.

Dust guided us to a small, tidy inn. It didn't look like the sort of place where you would normally find adventurers—more like a little hideaway for couples.

"This is it, Kazuma. This is where that walking pile of vomit brought Rin—like she was his toy!"

Hey, let's not be too hasty to pass judgment here…

Dust leaped to his feet. I started to worry that he might do something rash.

"So what have you got in mind?" I asked. "I assume you're not planning to just march right into the guy's room or anything, right?"

Dust grinned at me. "How long do you think I've been an adventurer? You want to survive in this business, you have to be prepared. I know exactly which room he's staying in, and I've already booked us the one next door."

Wh-whoa, now.

I had a mounting feeling that it might be best just to turn Dust in to the police right now, but he was already opening the door to the inn. I had no choice but to follow him. If he put this sort of persistence and initiative into his adventuring, he could probably achieve a lot more than he had…

The interior of the inn was done in the most basic possible style. On the first floor was a dining area, and on the second floor were the rooms. The owner saw us but didn't try to stop us; he just yawned in disinterest. Maybe it was because Dust had already made the arrangements.

Dust made a beeline for the second floor and finally came to a halt in front of one of the rooms.

"All right, this is it. The walls are thin here, so keep your voice down, okay? Rin should already be in the room next door. She's got sharp ears, so we have to be careful she doesn't hear us."

I nodded my understanding and followed Dust into the room. The furnishings were simple: a bed, a table, and a small dresser. Dust closed the door gently and then put his ear to the wall. I copied him, unable to shake the feeling that I was doing something I shouldn't be.

I heard a familiar girl's voice from the next room.

"I know, but… Having me do it would be really…"

That was Rin, no question. But it didn't sound like she was having a very good time.

"Rin, sweetheart, I know what I'm asking isn't easy. I know it would normally be taboo. But I can't help the love I feel!"

"C-calm down! You… You need to think this through. Nobles don't get involved with adventurers. That would be trouble enough…"

So he was an aristocrat. Rin could marry up! But from the way she was talking, it didn't sound like she was very excited at the prospect.

An adventurer and a son of the nobility. Normally, they would never even have seen each other on the street. That Darkness and I had ended up in a party together was the exception, not the rule.

As all this went through my head, the conversation on the other side of the wall continued.

"Rin, my dear! I'm painfully aware that the difference in status might make my feelings impossible to accept. And I know there are even greater obstacles to contend with. But at least… At least use this magic camera—this very *expensive* magic camera—to take a picture!"

"I said c-c-c-c-calm down! Take it easy already! Let's be rational!"

The conversation so far was enough to give us the gist of the situation. Some young noble had fallen head over heels for Rin, but the social distance between them was too great for them to be together. But what was this about "at least take a picture"? This guy didn't sound so bad.

"How can I?! How can I be rational when there is one who inflames me so?!"

"Look, just relax! Chill out! H-how about we go downstairs and have a little something to eat? To calm our nerves, okay?"

...All right. Maybe he wasn't the best guy in the world.

Beside me, Dust stood up with fire in his eyes.

"'Scuse me. I'm gonna beat the crap outta this guy."

"Hold on, don't do that! It's too soon!"

I somehow managed to restrain him. A moment later, we heard the door to the next room open, then shut again. They must have gone down to the first floor to eat.

Dust didn't say anything, but a nasty smile came over his face.

6

"Look at this, Kazuma! Clothes all over the floor! And fancy ones, too—he's a noble, all right!"

I had followed Dust directly into the other room. Now I was watching him turn the place inside out and fighting an increasing desire to put my head in my hands.

This time we've really gone too far.

Now we had added breaking and entering to the list of our crimes.

"All right, then. Let's see what that pampered prat's got in his—*Hey!* What's this?!"

I should really stop this.

I didn't want to compound my guilt with theft.

Dust had opened a dresser drawer and was looking into it in surprise. I had just placed a hand on his shoulder when—

"Look at this, Kazuma! Just look at this lacy red lingerie! That bastard was gonna force Rin to wear this and then take her picture! How perverse! How thoroughly prepared! Well, I'll show him what we do with crap like this!"

Then, without a moment's hesitation, he stripped naked and put on the lacy underwear himself.

No matter how perverted that noble might be, right at that moment, Dust was definitely worse.

"Okay, Kazuma! Grab that expensive-looking magic camera there and take a shot of me! We'll fill his precious film with boudoir photography of yours truly. Even if he did get a shot of Rin, this stuff'll make the whole experience so traumatic he'll never forget it!"

I have no idea what to say to this.

Feeling a bit overwhelmed, I did as I was told and picked up the camera. The construction looked fairly simple, but I could definitely feel a powerful magic within it. The object I was holding was probably worth as much as a house, and I was about to do the stupidest possible thing with it.

Dust stood there naked with his arms crossed, doing a backbend without even using his hands. He may have been a pervert, but he was also pretty built; he used his neck to support himself, forming a perfect arch with his toned body.

"Right! Do it, Kazuma! Now posterity can enjoy this beautiful body of mine!"

I lost track of how many photos I took. Dust smiled toothily into the camera from every angle: with me on the table looking down at him, from the floor looking up at him. We put that camera through its paces. *Pretend to be an eagle. Pretend to be a cougar. Pretend to be an artist thinking hard about his next piece.*

"Good stuff, Dust, keep it up! You're on fire, baby! That's it for the graceful beauty stuff—let's go for sexy beast next! Steeple your fingers and stick your butt out this way!"

Dust put his thumbs together as if he'd been a bad little boy and shoved his behind with those red panties in my direction. I hit the shutter a few times and then said, "That's the ticket! Cool's the word now! Legs wide, hips down, and hands—yes, that's it, just like that!"

He had adopted a sort of sumo-wrestler pose, his right hand stuck straight out in front of him. Wearing his most intense expression, he shouted the line I had taught him:

"Hakkeyoi!"

We were laughing so hard we were crying, clutching our sides. We could hardly take any more. We were rolling on the ground, slapping the floor in our mirth.

Thunk.

That was the sound of Rin standing in the open doorway, dropping her staff from sheer shock.

7

"So what's the story here?" Rin was asking. "I already know Dust is stupid enough to do something like this, but you, Kazuma?"

We were kneeling in front of Rin and the young nobleman.

""We're very sorry,"" we chorused.

We had gotten careless. It was like some weird switch had been flipped and we'd gotten completely caught up in taking ridiculous photos.

The pathetic sight of us was enough to provoke a long, deep sigh from Rin. The look she gave Dust was almost painful. Actually, so was seeing Dust in those red panties. I wished he would at least change his underwear.

"Gah," she said. "And here I was so worried about you. Do whatever you want with *him*; I won't stop you. Come on, Kazuma, let's go." Rin looked profoundly tired, but she held out a hand to me.

"Uh… Are you sure? Should we really leave those two together? Might turn into some real trouble…"

Rin took my hand and half dragged me outside.

"Don't worry about it. *I* certainly won't."

She shut the door with her free hand as we came out into the hall. We could still hear the voices of the two men still inside.

"Mr. Dust, you must understand that finding you in my room in such an outfit…"

"Oh? Yeah, I busted in. What are you gonna do, cry about it?"

It sounded like Dust was done being shaken and apologetic. Did he even understand what he looked like at that moment?

"Hey, Rin. Shouldn't you stop him? Something's gonna happen."

Rin, however, looked at me with tired eyes and shook her head in resignation. "Maybe he'll do something; maybe he'll have something done to him. I tried, Kazuma. I really tried. But then I open the door and there's that moron standing there, dressed like that… He's like a lobster who throws himself into the pot and closes the lid. There's nothing else I can do."

…?

Now, this was strange. I had the feeling we were talking past each other.

"O-obviously I'm not going to complain, Dust. Dust… Oh! Oh, Dust! Ahh, this is so…exciting! Rin told me to give up, but here you are… Thank the goddess I joined the Axis Church and kept praying and praying! There really *is* a deity in heaven!"

"I don't know what you're so thrilled about, but if you think I'm intimidated just because you're nobility, you're wrong. I'm totally used to being with kings or nobles or whoever. We're just two guys here, no more, no less. We clear on that?"

"Y-you mean you won't pay any heed to my status?! That here, we are simply two men?! Ahh… Ahhh! O Lady Aqua, I thank you for this most wonderful day!"

Rin and I left the inn without waiting to hear another word.

* * *

"So what were you two doing in a place like that anyway?" Rin asked, perplexed, as we came outside.

For a moment, I pondered whether to tell the truth, but then said, "Well, actually…"

I told her everything that had happened, emphasizing that Dust was genuinely worried about her.

The result was that Rin ended up laughing so hard she couldn't breathe.

"Ah— Ah-ha-ha—! Th-that buffoon! There's something wrong with the both of you! Ah-ha-ha-ha-ha!"

Believe me, I agree completely.

Frankly, I would never normally have gotten involved in something like this, but somehow Rin and Darkness just ran together in my mind…

Rin wiped away the tears from the corners of her eyes, but her shoulders were still shaking as she said:

"*Sigh*… You see, that nobleman? It's Dust he's really interested in."

At that, time stood still.

"……What?"

What had she just said?

"I told you: That nobleman came to me because he is in love with Dust and didn't know what to do. He understood that Dust wouldn't want to be with him, and he hoped I could at least take Dust's picture for him."

Then we heard it:

"Eeeeeeeeyyaaaaahhhhhhhh!"

A scream from Dust unlike any I had ever heard before, a sound like a dying bird from the second floor.

I had been considering Dust a temporary member of our party, but maybe it would be best to forget about that for a while. I walked along with Rin, trying to tell myself that nothing had happened today. I was exhausted; I just wanted to go home and take a nap.

I was trying to force my way through the mental haze to review my plans for the day when Rin said nonchalantly, "You know, that noble guy reminded me of something—it turns out our sweet Lalatina is a noble herself. I just found out recently. I had no idea!"

"That's some serious sleuthing. Who did you hear it from?" I asked.

Rin said only, "Everyone in town is talking about it. You know—how Lalatina is the daughter of the Dustiness family? How she's going to marry the local lord Alderp any day now?"

…………

"Details, please."

Chapter 4

May I Have One Last Night with This Noble Daughter!!

1

My voice was practically shaking as I declared to the two girls:

"And so we will now begin our strategy meeting regarding how to break in to a carefully guarded mansion and meet Darkness! Although I already have a pretty good idea!"

After I got home, I had explained the situation to Megumin and Aqua. Now the three of us were facing one another in the living room.

"Gosh, Kazuma, your voice is practically shaking," Aqua said. "Darkness's marriage to that lord who looks like the offspring of a pig and a bear is the talk of the town. I know Darkness has some strange tastes, but this is a bit too ridiculous even for her. Normally I would expect her father to put a stop to this. I wonder if something happened to him. I don't like this at all. Especially the fact that it's all just like that stinky, stupid demon predicted."

Aqua was sitting on the sofa, cradling her egg with an unusually serious face. It was true; Vanir had claimed that Darkness's family, including her father, would soon find themselves in trouble.

No normal person would believe in fortune-telling. It was half-truths at best. But this was a world with magic and curses.

"Do you believe that prediction, Kazuma? I see that despite your wealth, you've been industriously developing new products, just like that demon told you to. I hate demons less than Aqua does, but I agree that they help no one for free. All these predictions and warnings must benefit him somehow. If we could just go back to Crimson Magic Village, I have a friend who's a very experienced fortune-teller..."

I didn't know what to say to Megumin, because I didn't know how I felt. Granted, I wasn't sure it was wise to go around believing everything a demon told you. And yet...

"I don't think Vanir is just making things up, although I'm sure he's not telling us the whole truth, either. I don't know what benefit it is to him if we rescue Darkness. Look, guys, I won't try to pretend anymore. The reason I've been working so hard on new products is because I hoped, if something really did happen to Darkness, that one of them might help us help her. Anyway, it's not like I have anything to lose from a little research and development, even if the prediction doesn't come true. That's all I was really thinking..."

Darkness wasn't the sharpest knife in the drawer, and she had probably done this impulsively, thinking that if she sacrificed herself, everything would be better. That was what Vanir had told Darkness in his prediction. If I had just heard it from some random palm reader on the street, I might have forgotten about it. But this...

"Whatever the case, there are a lot of things we can't be sure about yet," I said. "For now it's just thirdhand information, something Rin told us she heard. We have to get in touch with Darkness and talk to her ourselves if we want to know what's going on. Her letter only said she was leaving the party, so I didn't want to pry into her business too much, but we've had our fair share of trouble at Alderp's hands. We need to talk to Darkness and find out what's happening, even if we have to force our way inside. What do you say? Are you with me?"

Carried along by my enthusiasm, Megumin and Aqua nodded intently.

I recalled our (former) resident idiot saying at one point that as noble marriage prospects went, Alderp was enough of a sleazebag to rate a "not bad" from her. I hated to say it, but we couldn't even completely rule out the possibility that something had happened to her father and Darkness had initiated the marriage proposal herself.

She really could say the stupidest things sometimes. Like when she tried to foist herself on Beldia, or the time she was thrilled to be possessed by Vanir. Or the time when we were on our way to Crimson Magic Village and she was really and truly shocked to learn that the male orcs had all been wiped out.

And then there was the way she ushered herself out of our party with nothing but a letter. Now that I thought about it, she had caused us an awful lot of worry during our time together.

But whatever. In this case, we had to get the details straight from the Crusader's mouth. While we were at it, I figured I would ask her what was up with that letter.

I wasn't eager to go demand to know what was happening on just the strength of a letter, but after what Rin had said, what choice did I really have?

Right… What choice at all?

I swear I wasn't in the least bit thinking about a chance to get revenge for all the anxiety I'd suffered. I definitely wasn't a little excited at the thought of breaking into the Dustiness mansion or because this was the perfect pretext to see *her* again.

Oh-ho, Darkness, just you wait…

I was just sitting there thinking. Why was Megumin smiling at me? Even Aqua looked as if she was seeing something unusual.

Finally, she said, "Hey, Kazuma. You've been so crabby lately. Right now you finally look…happy."

She sounded almost pleased about it.

2

"All right. Now's the perfect time. Aqua, if you please."

The time, specifically, was two o'clock in the morning. We were at the Dustiness mansion, though not at the closely watched front or back gates. We were off to one side, where there was no entryway at all.

An iron fence surrounded the entire mansion. I was peeking in between the bars from a shadowy spot on the road.

At my signal, Aqua began quietly chanting some magic spells. Buffs, support magic. Incantations to strengthen my body and muscle me up. I even had her raise my physical and magical defenses, although I didn't know if I would need them.

Then she intoned a spell I didn't recognize.

"*Versatile Entertainer*!"

A pale light surrounded me for a moment. Was this another buff?

"What's that one do?"

"It makes you a better artiste," she said.

Without a word, I gave her a smack. I ignored her tearful attempt to strangle me in return; instead, I pulled a bow from my back. My arrows were tipped with hooks, like the ones we had used so successfully against Mobile Fortress Destroyer. The ends were wrapped in cloth so they wouldn't make a sound when I launched them onto the roof.

"Okay, here goes."

After some discussion, the two of us had decided that I should go in alone. I was the one with Ambush and plenty of other skills suited for infiltration, like the one that let me see in the dark. Sure, this was a noble's mansion, but I had broken into a royal castle before. This was nothing.

I wasn't looking to hurt anyone, so I didn't bring any gear besides my bow. And even that I would hand off to Aqua to take home after I had set my arrows in place.

"Remember the mission," Aqua whispered. "Knock out Darkness and kidnap her!"

"Sh-should a member of the clergy really be saying that sort of thing?"

"She is right," Megumin piped up. "Darkness being who she is, I'm sure she will be stubborn about telling us what's going on. Feel free to be a little rough with her if you need to!"

"Why are you both so excited about this?"

As Aqua and Megumin looked on, I readied an arrow and used the Deadeye skill to launch it as close to the top of the roof as I could. My aim was true: There was a soft *click* as it caught on an edge. We all stood frozen for a moment, but nobody seemed to have noticed the sound.

I tied the rope to one of the bars of the iron fence, then I said to the girls, "Untie that once I get to the roof. If any guards notice this rope, they'll know someone's broken in. You guys go back to the mansion and wait. I'll figure out some way to get home."

They nodded. I gave the rope another tug to be sure it was secure.

Okay! Time to get this show on the road.

I worked my way smoothly up the rope as if I were an Army Ranger. With my usual perfectly average physical strength, it would have been a challenge, but Aqua's strength-enhancing buffs came to my aid.

I got up on the roof, then signaled to Aqua. Down below, I saw her undo the rope. I used my Sense Foe skill to check if there was anyone around. It also helped me locate a nice empty room inside the house. I intended to use the rope still dangling from the roof to enter the room from a second-floor window, but I found the window locked.

Times like this, however, were when my modern-day knowledge came into play.

"*Kindle.*"

I clung to the rope with one hand, creating a flame with the other and passing it over the glass. There was no fuel around, so my MP limited the amount of fire I could make, but I produced one flame after another. Finally, the glass was hot enough…

"*Freeze,*" I whispered. The temperature of the glass plummeted, and it shattered with a gentle tinkling. I kept watch to see if the noise had attracted anyone's attention, but it didn't look like it.

The old burn-and-bust was a classic way of breaking and entering, although it usually involved a lighter and some water. I had learned about the method on the Net back when I was in my full-on fantasy-escapism phase, during which time I was interested in collecting dangerous knowledge I had no intention of using. Who knew the random trivia I'd absorbed back then would come in handy one day?

I fit some fingers into the newly made hole, then wiggled my hand, clearing the glass around the lock bit by bit. Finally I had a hole big enough to undo the latch; I popped the window open and slipped inside.

Now I was safely in. The question was how to find Darkness's room.

Should I sneak into the hallway and check each room individually? No—even with my Ambush skill, the chance of being spotted by a guard was too high. Well, what about—?

"Did you hear something?"

"Don't think so. I hope you were only imagining it..."

The voices were just outside the door. In a panic, I closed the curtain to conceal the broken window and swept up the shards of glass on the carpet. I could hear the key in the lock as I dove under the bed and activated Ambush.

Then I heard the door open, followed by a voice that was at once relieved and exasperated. "See, Norris? It's nothing. You have to get over that anxious streak of yours. Well, forget it. Let's hit the kitchen and you can make me something to eat."

"I-I'm sorry. I was sure I heard something breaking..."

The door closed, and the men's footsteps receded down the hall. I didn't move a muscle. Given what they had said about eating in the kitchen, they were probably a couple of the mansion's guards. That definitely nixed the idea of checking every room.

How about this, then? I head to the kitchen those guards mentioned; announce that the young lady, Lalatina, has asked for food; then trail them right back to her room!

Okay, there were all kinds of problems with that plan. I couldn't let anyone see my face, and I didn't think I was enough of a vocalist to impersonate one of those guards.

I'll bet Aqua could pull it off, what with all her stupid party tricks…

Party tricks.

I had an idea. That one guard, his name was Norris, right? I cleared my throat.

"My name…is…Norris?" I said, trying to sound like the guard. I was astonished by how convincing my own imitation was. I sounded so much like him that it actually creeped me out a little. I had been sort of curious to try out the entertainer buff Aqua had cast on me earlier.

"*O-oh no, this is bad…* Yes! It's Darkness. Definitely Darkness. No matter how you slice it, it's Darkness!" I could even imitate *her* voice!

Perfect! I could make use of this! I would have to apologize to Aqua when I got home.

……

"My God, Kazuma, you're amazing! Make love to me!"

I spent a moment having a little fun with the voices of Darkness and my other companions until, with a start, I realized I didn't have time for this. I was in danger of losing sight of my objective. I had never wanted a tape recorder more in my life—but right now the important thing was to find my Crusader.

I decided to start with the kitchen. I crept out of the room and made sure Ambush was still active…

I tailed Norris and his friend to the kitchen. After I was sure they were gone, I went up to the door. I cleared my throat and thought of Norris's voice. Then I gave a hurried knock on the door and started yammering:

"I'm sorry, it's me, Norris! I forgot, the young lady asked me to bring her dinner! I have to get back to my post—please ask someone to take her food to her!"

I mentally apologized to Norris, whom I had never even met.

The voice on the other side of the door was almost wry. "Hell, Norris, you're always so much trouble. Jumpy *and* forgetful! Fine, we'll make sure she gets it. Get back to work."

"Thank you!" I said, trying to sound as rushed as I could. "You're the best!" Then I made a show of noisily scrambling away.

In fact, however, I ducked behind some nearby furniture and waited for the kitchen staff to come out. I had waited quite a while when I finally sensed someone emerging from the kitchen…

3

"Young Lady, I brought your dinner," the staff member said, knocking on a door. I watched him from the shadows.

So that's Darkness's room. Excellent.

The guy knocked several times before the door finally opened. It looked like Darkness had already gone to sleep. She was wearing a dark-blue negligee, and her hair was loose. She rubbed her eyes as she poked her head out of the room.

The staff guy quickly looked away. "Erm, *Norris* said you'd requested something to eat."

Darkness gave him a sleepy look. "I don't recall doing that."

Startled, the kitchen guy bowed his head. "I-I'm very sorry, then, ma'am. My apologies for bothering you so late!" He excused himself as quickly as he could. Darkness, still looking a bit perplexed, closed the door.

The staff member, hanging his head, walked right past where I was hiding. A little while later, confident no one else was coming, I knocked on the door of Darkness's room.

"Young Lady, please wake up. I know how late it is, but a man named Kazuma Satou has appeared and is demanding an audience with you," I said in Norris's voice. A moment later, I heard movement from inside…

"I thought I told you," came Darkness's voice, "if anyone named Kazuma, Aqua, or Megumin comes asking for me, you are absolutely not to let them in. And in the middle of the night, for crying out loud... Oh, for...for Eris's sake...!" It sounded like it hurt her to say this, but like she was also secretly happy.

"But, Young Lady," I replied, still in the guard's voice, "this Mr. Kazuma said that if we didn't let him in, he would reveal all of Miss Lalatina's dirty secrets to the entire Guild..."

I could hear a happy laugh at that. "Heh! He hasn't changed," Darkness said. Then her voice grew quieter. "Tell Kazuma he can do whatever he likes. They'll never see me at the Adventurers Guild again anyway."

......

"But, Young Lady, at this very moment that man is in the front hall, spreading untoward rumors among the staff. He claims that your abs have become too ripped lately, and that's why you've refused protein in your meals."

I heard a clatter.

"Also, he says that not long ago you were in an adorable dress, smiling, and he hopes we will ready such clothes for you now."

I heard another clatter. It seemed to be the sound of something breaking. Then came Darkness's voice, shaking violently. "Th-th-th-th-those rumors are just lies! Made up! Pure fiction! Tell the staff not to be taken in by his stories!"

....

"Truth be told, he's saying even worse things. May I repeat them, Young Lady?"

After a moment, Darkness said, "Let me hear it."

I took a deep breath. "He alleges that although the young lady is a virgin, night after night her untrammeled sexual urges cause her to—"

The door flew open, and there was Darkness, cheeks burning and tears in her eyes.

Then our gazes met.

"?!!?????!??!??"

Her eyes were the size of dinner plates, her mouth working open and shut.

Got her!

4

I clapped my hand over Darkness's mouth and pushed her backward into the room. Eyes wide, she grabbed my hand with both of hers and tried to pull me off.

"I've got Aqua's strength buffs on me—you won't get rid of me that easily!" I hissed in her ear. I used my free hand to shut and lock the door. The sound of the key in the lock caused Darkness to spasm for some reason.

I kept one hand tight over her mouth so she couldn't cry out. With my other hand, I grabbed her right wrist, then I did a quick scan of the room. It was dark, presumably because she'd been asleep until a second ago. Only starlight, filtering in through the window, illuminated us. Was I going to have to pin her to the floor to get her to listen to me?

Then I noticed the big bed behind her. Summoning all my enhanced strength, I lifted Darkness up.

"?!"

I was pretty sure she never expected weak li'l ol' me to pick her up with one arm. Maybe Aqua really wanted me to bring Darkness home, because her buffs today were above and beyond.

With one great bound, I shoved Darkness onto the bed. There was a gentle *fwump* as she sank into the mattress. I inserted myself between her legs, taking care not to get kicked.

Good. Now we can finally talk without her fighting m—?

Darkness let all the strength out of the hand that had been gripping my arm, letting it flop down onto the bed. Tears were beading at the corners of her moist eyes, and in the faint light of the stars, I could see her cheeks were flushed. Her flustered breaths trickled out between the fingers of the hand I still had clapped over her mouth.

...Whaaa...?!

Hang on, this was one dangerous situation! How about some resistance? A little more fight? *What am I gonna do if you just let me have my way?!*

With Aqua's wholehearted support magic behind me, I didn't think I would lose to Darkness in a contest of strength. But now that she was looking totally defenseless and resigned like this... Well, that caused its own problems!

In the quiet shadows, I whispered, "H-hey, Darkness, don't get the wrong idea, okay? I know this is one hundred percent weird, but it's just— You know. I only came here to talk to you, so don't think I'm trying to break into your room for...any other reason, all right? H-hey! Open those eyes! Don't act all resigned to your fate! Stop it! You're making this way more awkward than it has to be! Stop it, I said! This is—this is all kinds of dangerous!"

Dangerous for who? Dangerous for me. If I went back and said I broke into her room so I could talk to her, but she was so hot that I just got carried away and crossed *that* line... I think it would be a vicious cycle of Explosion and Resurrection for as long as they could manage.

I shook Darkness violently, keeping my hand over her mouth.

"Fine, then just lie there and listen to me! I busted in here so I could ask you what the hell is going on, okay? I'm going to take my hand away now. Don't shout or anything. I've only come to talk, all right?"

My pleading caused Darkness to open her eyes slightly and nod.

Phew...

For some reason, I was more nervous than I had ever been in any of our battles.

"All right, I'm letting go now. Remember, no screaming."

Darkness nodded again. I positioned myself so I could slap my hand back down if she started to yell, then slowly pulled my hand away.

Free of my grip, Darkness turned her head to one side as if she was embarrassed.

"You think...maybe you could look away, too, Kazuma? Are we really going to have a conversation staring into each other's eyes from this close? In this position?"

I quickly looked in the opposite direction from Darkness. "Y-yeah, sure, you're right. S-sorry I couldn't find us a better place to chat! But why would you leave us a letter like that anyway?"

No sooner had I let my attention slip away from Darkness than she exclaimed, "Perrrverrrt! I'm being atta— Hrmgh!"

Argh! She got me! Dammit, I can't believe I let my guard down!

I shoved my hand back over her mouth, but it was too little, too late. I could already hear a commotion from the hallway. Somebody was coming this way, fast.

Crap, crap, crap, what am I gonna do?!

Although she was once again silenced, Darkness looked up at me with a taunting triumph in her eyes. The laughter in her expression was unmistakable.

Stupid, stupid Darkness!

"What's the matter, Young Lady?! I'm going to open the door now!"

A key scraped in the lock...

Gaaah! How I hate that victorious look on her face! But if she thinks I'm out of ideas, she's got another think coming...

"No, don't! I'm not decent! I'm sorry—I was just, uh, playing, and I got so excited I couldn't contain myself and cried out!"

When she heard my voice, Darkness's eyes got huge. That's right: I was impersonating her.

"Er... But I really must confirm your safety, miss. And what do you mean by 'playing' at this time of night anyway?"

He didn't believe me. I didn't blame him; he probably thought the invader had forced Darkness to say all that.

"Playing! You know, as...as adults sometimes do, at night, by themselves... Don't make me say more; it's too embarrassing!"

"Young Lady…?!" The voice on the other side of the door choked.

At the same moment, Darkness grabbed my right hand with her free one.

"Or perhaps…," I said, "…is checking on me just some sad excuse to see me in my least presentable state? You twisted perrrrrvert!"

Darkness, staring daggers at me while tears flew from her eyes, gripped my arm so hard she seemed ready to break it. It was enough to send my voice up an octave, at which the panicked interrogation from the hallway resumed.

"Wh-what's going on in there?!"

Fighting against the pain, I replied, "N-nothing! I just forgot to turn off this strange magical toy! Ahhh! Oh! I'm gonna break! I'm going nuts! Any more, and I'll—I'll really break!"

"P-pardon me, Young Lady! I m-m-must excuse myself!"

The footsteps rushed back down the hall. Darkness's shouting (or rather, my shouting in her voice) seemed to have attracted a small crowd, but whatever the guy said to them, I sensed them dispersing.

Somehow I withstood the pain in my arm; I looked down at Darkness, who was quaking and crying, and smirked at her.

5

Darkness started jabbing at the hand I had over her mouth. She seemed to be saying, *I won't scream again, so let me go.* When I finally pulled my hand away, she let out a deep breath.

I looked at the arm Darkness had grabbed and saw a huge hand-shaped bruise. Without Aqua's defensive buffs, it probably really would have broken.

In an exasperated tone, Darkness said, "Sheesh. You're as awful as ever. Now look what you've done. Every servant in the household is going to think I'm some weirdo who— Hmm—?!"

That was as far as she got before she started shuddering.

"You're thinking that wouldn't be half bad, aren't you?"

"Am not."

"Are too."

A time like this, and she *still*— Sigh.

"All right, spill it," I said. "What's with leaving the party? Aqua and Megumin are worried sick about you, you know. You at least owe us an explanation. We're—"

—your friends is what I was about to say, but I suddenly felt embarrassed to act so…involved.

Darkness, as if oblivious to my feelings, only laughed. "There are some things I can't tell you *because* you're my friends. It's nothing all that important anyway. Just a family matter. This household borrowed money from that lord. My father was supposed to repay it a little bit at a time. But he hasn't been in the best of health lately, so Alderp has started pressing the matter. He wants to know if my father can really repay him before he dies. He also said that if I would marry him, he would forgive the debt. That's it. That's the whole story."

"That's it," my ass.

"You mean your family is in *debt* to that moron? Hang on, I thought your dad was supposed to be some kind of VIP in this country. Couldn't he go to the king for money? And anyway, it's almost—" I snapped my mouth shut.

Almost like…

"Like I'm being sold to pay my father's debt? Yes, that's exactly what it is. But that's not so strange among noble houses. The daughter of one family is sent as a bride to another. It's nothing more than that." Darkness sounded as if it really was nothing to her. When she saw my expression, she went on. "Don't make that face, Kazuma. You know what kind of men I like. I think that lord wants to make me his own the moment he gets the chance. He's shoved aside all kinds of traditional ceremonies to hurry up the wedding day. He's so frustrated, I don't think he'll even be able to wait for our first night together. He looks like he might just take me in a back room somewhere. Heh! Do you think he might starve me? Refuse to give me food or water? It's enough to make my heart pound…!"

She laughed. She was trying to fool me. Pretend it was a joke… Well, if it was as funny as that, why did she look so sad?

"So that was why you were so hell-bent on us defeating the hydra by ourselves. And I had to go and get all those people involved… How much is this debt? I could—"

"Please don't say you'll pay, Kazuma. I'm a noble. Nobles are supposed to protect the common people. Have a commoner repay my debt using money he earned at the risk of his life? I would sooner choose to sell myself. Anyway, it doesn't matter. The debt is so large that even your current resources couldn't cover it." She stared straight at me as she spoke.

I was still on top of her. In the starlight, I took a fresh look at Darkness, whom I hadn't seen in so long. Her proud, stubborn blue eyes gazed back at me. Her golden hair was splayed across the bed, glowing faintly in the reflected light from the heavens. Her breathing still wasn't quite under control from the struggle earlier, and a bead of sweat dribbled down her cheek.

With each hard inhale and exhale, her chest, covered only by her sheer nightgown, rose and fell, making its presence inescapably obvious. The fight with me had caused the straps of her negligee to fall down off her shoulders. Her whole body was warm…

Panicked, I mentally intoned some magic spells to help clear my head.

My mom half-naked, rolling around in the living room…

When I realized that underwear belonged to my grandmother…

Dust's butt in red panties…!

I beg of you all, give this heart of mine a moment's peace!

The magic had its effect; I was startlingly calm. Right, now I could deal with this a little longer.

Looking up at me, Darkness smiled gently and whispered, "Can you imagine stealing such a rich prize right from under Alderp's nose?

How about it, Kazuma? It's just the two of us. Shall we make adults out of each other?"

The magic suddenly stopped working.

Calm down, Kazuma Satou! Think!

Darkness is just saying that because she's all set to be a bride. She's given up; she doesn't believe she'll ever see me again.

It can't end like this, can it?

No, it can't. I'll never let someone like him *have her.*

That meant it wouldn't be right to cross that final line here and now. What, was I ready to be Darkness's boyfriend?

Hell no! Get it together, Kazuma Satou! Remember what you came here to do!

As I tried to keep myself from falling apart, Darkness gently took my hand and began drawing it closer to her body…

She seemed to be at a loss where exactly to go with it. Maybe she couldn't quite bring herself to put it directly on her chest.

I looked at her anxious face, hesitated for about two seconds, and then…!

I decided not to worry about what came next and just let the moment sweep me along.

Darkness put my hand gently on her stomach and shivered. She closed her eyes. I knew this was the time to say something really smooth. I ran my hand over her pale, supple skin and said…

"Wow. Your abs really are ripped."

6

Darkness and I faced each other in the star-washed room.

Her eyes were bulging and her fists were up, ready to fight. What had happened to the sexy times I was about to have?

"I'm sorry! I said I'm sorry! I just wasn't thinking! Geez, I couldn't stand it any longer!"

"I'm not always just playing at being upset, you know! You have a woman who's ready to give herself to you, who's totally committed, and you humiliate her like that?! Don't think you're going to get off so easily. You'll be lucky if you get off *alive*!"

"Young Lady," I said, "such base threats are beneath a woman of your station." Then I dropped the fancy-butler act and said, "Geez. If you were in love with me, why didn't you just say so?!"

"Who said anything as stupid as that, you big, dumb stupid-head?! Now I'm *really* angry! And stop calling me 'Young Lady'!"

Darkness flew at me even as she shouted. My speed was buffed like everything else, and I easily avoided her.

I heard footsteps in the hall again. That was it. We could only make so much noise in the middle of the night before there was no more throwing them off.

"Ha-ha! How about that, Kazuma? The house staff is on the way! If they find you in here, believe me, you'll suffer. Forcing your way into a noblewoman's bedroom? If I don't intercede for you, all the smooth talk in the world won't keep your head on your shoulders. So how about a little kowtow and a nice heartfelt apology?"

Apparently, my avoiding her attack had pissed her off even worse. I could practically see the steam coming out her ears. I could sense a whole crowd outside, and there was a fevered pounding on the door.

"Young Lady! Young Lady, we're coming in now!"

Darkness held her arms wide, preparing to grab, and then she jumped at me. Even under normal circumstances I wouldn't have had any real trouble getting away from her, but with Aqua's spells, there was no way I could lose.

And all this after I had worried and worked so hard to get here. If she thought I was going to give up now and beg for help, boy was she wrong!

"Come at me, Erosader! That's right—you've got nothing but your hot body and your stamina and your muscles! I'm from the weakest class of all, and I can overpower you! Can and will—and I'll leave you a crying wreck, just you watch! You saw me get serious back in the capital—you want some more of that?"

I said every word of this in Darkness's own voice. Then I caught her hands in mine and we leaned into each other.

"D-don't you steal my voice!"

"Y-Young Lady?! What on earth are you doing in there?!" The voice on the other side of the door sounded very confused. Fair enough: Darkness and I did sound identical now.

The key scrabbled in the lock. I glanced toward the door and shouted, "No, you mustn't open it! Your sweet Lalatina isn't wearing a shred of clothing! You mustn't look at meeee!"

"Whaaa—?! S-sorry!"

For a second, the key went silent. I took the opportunity to use Drain Touch on Darkness, stealing her vitality. But she was a cut above mere royal knights; a quick Drain didn't even make her flinch. She just gripped my hands even harder, her face turning red.

"Spare me this 'you mustn't' nonsense! In my own voice, no less! Hey, don't listen to him! He's an invader, using magic to make himself sound like me!"

"Y-yes, miss! Right away, miss!"

The key started up again.

Damn it all!

"Ha-ha-ha-ha-ha! Victory goes to me this time, Kazuma! I haven't always bested you in our battles, but how satisfying to triumph this one last time!"

I was draining her even as she spoke, but she was holding her ground.

One last time? Screw that! Now I'm really *not gonna lose!*

I let myself go limp; Darkness, who had been leaning into me, pitched forward. I took the opportunity to free my left hand and slammed it down on her back.

I didn't make any effort to sound like anyone but myself as I bellowed, "*Freeze*!!"

"Nnngaahh!"

Darkness yelled and quaked as the ice magic suddenly assaulted her skin. Her face was still flushed and her body still trembling as she collapsed to her knees. I wrenched my right hand away from her, and—

"Young Lady!" The door flew open with a *bang*, but I was already pointing my palm in the direction of the entryway.

"*Create Earth*!"

It was the simple blinding tactic I so often used. When Darkness saw the pile of dust in my hand, she knew exactly what I was planning and tried to warn the staff.

"Everyone cover your—"

—*eyes!* is what she was going to say, but I was too fast.

"*Wind Breath*!"

A magical gust sprang up.

7

Kazuma here.

I'm an adventurer from Japan.

My dream is to live free and easy with so much money that I never have to worry about anything again. It's a simple dream, and until this moment, I have lived a life of peace.

"Did you find him?! He's not in the shadows over here! Our enemy has the Ambush skill, so be sure to check even the dark corners where nothing appears to be! Capture him—do *not* let him get away! In the name of the Dustiness family, I charge you to find that man and bring him to me!"

""""Yes, ma'am!!""""

At that moment, I was trying desperately to figure out a way to put some distance between me and Darkness, who had well and truly lost her mind.

"Kazumaaaaa! Where are you? If you turn yourself in like a grown-up, I'll let you off with ten of my full-strength punches. But if I have to find you myself, you'll have it way worse than that."

Darkness, veins bulging as she shouted, was standing directly behind me. I was crouched down with Ambush on, creeping along the hallway.

It looked like every ounce of blood in Darkness's body had gone to her head. She was in no fit state to talk, so I was going to call it a night. Anyway, I had a feeling that if she caught me now, she might legitimately kill me—knowing that Aqua could just resurrect me again.

I ducked into a nearby room, one that I thought might conceal a way out of the house. Luckily for me, the door wasn't locked.

Okay. Now out the window…

Just as I was creeping toward my exit, a small voice came from the bed in the middle of the room.

"Is… Is someone there…?"

It was Darkness's father. Even in the poorly lit bedchamber, I could see how thin his cheeks were, how pale his skin had gotten.

"Oh, it's you…," he whispered. "Imagine, seeing you here in the middle of the night… I see… My daughter has truly been blessed with fine friends…" His bony cheeks lifted in a smile.

Apparently, my mere presence was enough for him to figure out what I was there for. I guess they didn't call him the kingdom's confidant for nothing.

Even so, he looked nothing like he had the last time we'd met. He had been so full of life; now he smiled weakly. What kind of illness could ravage a man so quickly?

Footsteps hurried down the hallway.

"Sir, I'm sorry to ask a favor when you're so ill, but your daughter is very, very angry right now. Do you think you could talk her down for me?"

The old man laughed merrily from his bed. "Is that right? She's kept herself locked away in her room for so long. Is she finally feeling well enough to get angry?"

I really don't think most fathers would laugh at that.

...And I had a thought.

"Sir. I've heard the story—how this family is indebted to Lord Alderp. But I have trouble believing someone like you would ever borrow money from someone like him. And your lifestyle doesn't look that extravagant, either. So why the debt...?"

This was my chance to question Darkness's father about the things that had been bothering me. I felt bad interrogating him when he was in such poor health, but Darkness wouldn't tell me what was going on; maybe her dad would.

"...Mm. Young Kazuma," he said after a moment, "I knew you were intelligent. Perhaps I really shall entrust my daughter to you. I'm very sorry, but...please take her. Take her and run away somewhere safe."

What the heck was he talking about? I ask him about a debt, and he tells me to elope with his daughter?

"I'll pass, thanks. That one's a miss for sure. In fact, it so happens that I'm in this room because I'm trying to run away *from* your daughter. Very ladylike young woman you've raised there."

"Ha-ha! Indeed. Ladylike and kind. Purehearted and shy, and loath to cause anyone trouble."

He ignored my sarcasm and even seemed to be proud of his daughter. Whatever was making him sick, it looked like it had affected his brain. I wanted to ask him if we were talking about the same person, but I kept my mouth shut.

Darkness's dad looked right at me. His body might have been wasting away, but there was still a powerful light in his eyes.

"Please don't ask me why. My daughter knew about the debt when I entered into it, but— Well, if she isn't here, then that's that. I can sell the house; it will bring a fair amount. Anyway, I'm exploring various possibilities. The debt itself may yet disappear."

So… Did that mean the debt was unjust? Whatever. Dad was capable enough to take care of that.

"It's my daughter. She's the one who's rushing to give herself away. I wish only that she be stopped. Young Kazuma, if I understand correctly, my daughter does not think ill of you. Perhaps my pride misleads me, but I believe she is a worthy young woman herself… Do you agree?"

"Oh. Uh, what a question. She just told me a few minutes ago that she was going to murder me." Anyway, there was something more important to deal with now. "Tell me what's wrong with you. We have an excellent Arch-priest… Er, well, excellent at magic anyway. She can even use Resurrection. I don't know what's ailing you, but I'll bring her here."

Darkness's father just smiled faintly at that. "No… It's hopeless. Illness can't be cured with healing magic, and those who die of illness can't be brought back with Resurrection. Sickness has to do with our allotted life spans. No miracle can touch those who have lived out their lives. Whatever the cause of our end, we should be happy to run our race and go to the gods. So you needn't look so somber."

I hadn't realized I had let my thoughts into my expression.

"Could you at least let our Arch-priest look at you? I mean, for your health to fail right at this particular moment…"

"You suspect His Lordship has poisoned me?" Dad finished the thought before I could.

…That was exactly what I suspected.

I had seen how Alderp lusted after Darkness. It was completely plausible that he was behind this…

"I've already investigated the possibility. It was the first thing I did. But there was no sign of poison."

…I knew he was a sharp one. He had probably considered scenarios that hadn't even occurred to me.

"*Still?!* You still haven't found him?! Kazuma, get out here! And explain to these people that you were just imitating my voice! I didn't say those things!"

A wry smile crossed Darkness's father's face when he heard his daughter in the hallway.

"I'm asking you… Take care of her."

N-no thanks… Really…

"Can't you ask the king to intercede on your behalf or something? You're a big deal in this country, right? If Alderp is trying to stick you with an unjust debt…"

The old man closed his eyes and shook his head gently. "Perhaps I could, but my daughter would still end up married to him. Where did she get such tenacity? If I went to the king, my daughter would only chastise me for using the people's taxes in such a way and insist that she go to wife to settle the debt." He paused, then murmured, "How did I raise someone so uncomprehending?"

My question exactly, sir. Ex-act-ly.

I really wished he could do something about his stubborn daughter…

At just that moment, the door flew open, and there was Darkness, nostrils flared, glaring in our direction.

"Heh-heh-heh… So this is where you've been hiding. Ha-ha-ha! Now, what am I going to do with you…?"

"Hey," I said, "there's a sick man here. Keep your voice down. And get your head together already. I came here on behalf of the party because we were worried about you!"

Darkness showed no sign of having heard me; she looked like a woman possessed. "No excuses! For someone who's worried about me, you sure succeeded in destroying my reputation in record time! This is a matter between noble houses. A commoner like you shouldn't get involved. Go back to your mansion and make some more of your weird little toys!"

Why, this obnoxious—!

"Forget about the stupid debt already!" I said. "Why can't we just run away from it?! Why can't we all just start over somewhere new? Anyway, you know as well as I do that if I slink back home without you, those two—especially Megumin!—are gonna do something terrible for sure! Don't be surprised if the whole ceremony goes down the tubes on your wedding day!"

"Just you try it—I'll have them arrested, and you as a coconspirator! Don't like it? Then keep a leash on your party! I'm not going to run away! If I did, the burden would just fall on someone else! Forget it, you and I have other business—!"

Then she charged at me. It looked like she was bent on settling our score before she got married.

Crap, she's really gonna murder me!

I spun on my heel and made for the window.

"You stupid, dense, obtuse—! Fine! Do whatever you want! But don't think I'll be there for you when you get all weepy!" I aimed a flying kick at the glass portal. "You want my help, feel free to come by the mansion and apologize! *I'm so sorry for worrying you, dear, sweet Kazuma!* you'll say! *Please, please help m*— Grrf!"

The window glass was stronger than I'd expected, and it failed to give way under my kick. I had to body-slam it to get it to shatter, but that threw me off balance, and I went tumbling to the ground.

We were just a couple of stories up, but with no chance to break my fall, I slammed into the ground—never a pleasant experience. Darkness ran to the window and looked down at me.

"A-are you all right, *dear, sweet* Kazuma?! If you apologize—*I'm very sorry, Lady Dustiness; please help me*—we won't begrudge you healing!"

Her shoulders were shaking. She was barely restraining her laughter. I forced my body to move, starting to climb the iron fence to escape the guards who were coming this way after the commotion.

"D-damn you, Darkness! I'll never help you again unless you apologize to me with tears in your eyes! Argh, stay back! *Create Water*! *Freeze*!"

As I tried to get in a final parting shot at Darkness, who was watching all this with glee, I laid down a trap for my pursuers and fled for my mansion.

8

"Hrrgh-gh-gh-gh! Aqua! Aquaaaaa! Heal me! Heal me right nowwwww!"

I barely understood how I made it back to the mansion. I went up to Aqua, who was dozing on the living room sofa, her egg in her hands. Darkness hadn't pursued me to the house, maybe because she couldn't stand the thought of seeing Aqua or Megumin.

"...*Yawn*. Huh? Kazuma, you're a mess! Were you able to see Darkness? How did you end up like that? Did you say something stupid again?" Aqua used some healing magic as she fired questions at me.

Wait... Why does she look sort of...happy to see me like this?

Our conversation woke up Megumin, who was sleeping on the sofa next to Aqua.

"Welcome back, Kazuma. Whatever happened to you? Did you say something foolish again? Were you able to convince Darkness to come home?"

Now I know how you two see me.

Aqua's magic made my injuries better in a flash, but it couldn't do anything about the empty feeling in my heart. Still frustrated and indignant, I headed for my room on the second floor.

"Forget about that jerk," I said. "Unless she comes crying, ignore her! I don't know what's going to happen to her—and I don't care."

Aqua and Megumin looked at each other.

"Aww... But Darkness and I had a promise to build a little house for Zel when he hatches..." She looked down sadly at her egg.

Megumin said, "I don't know what happened, Kazuma, but is this really the time to pout? Do you at least know why Darkness has to get married?"

I stopped on the stairway. "Debt. Her family owes a bunch of money! And if she marries Alderp, he'll forget all about it!"

"Erk… Debt?" Megumin said. "I don't know how much she owes, but I've already sent money back to my family, so I don't have very much on me right now…" She looked into her wallet, which was stuffed with coupons and membership cards, and let out an anxious sigh.

"Well, you know what they say about a friend in need," Aqua added. "If she really needs money that badly, I can break open my piggy bank."

Sure, like that would help.

I didn't know how much the Dustinesses owed, but if it was enough that Darkness had to get married to settle the debt, then it was a lot. More than Megumin and Aqua could make up with their pocket change.

I turned my back on them and resumed the trek to my room. "She's decided what she wants to do. Leave her alone and let her do it! Either she comes back here weeping and apologizing, or I forget I ever knew her."

"Kazuma, this isn't the time for theatrics!" Megumin said to my back. "Darkness is going to be married off! Can you really live with that?!"

Why don't you ask her*?!*

Chapter 5 God's Blessing on This Beautiful Bride!

1

The town had been one big party for several days now. The normally stingy Lord Alderp had spread a little wealth around the city, hoping to create some excitement about his upcoming wedding. It was like he was trying to make it that much harder for anyone involved to change their minds.

The date was set and had already been announced: The ceremony was to take place in a week. I guess he really *couldn't* wait. I was sure he was busy getting all hot and bothered at the thought of the day he could finally marry Darkness.

"Kazuma, I ask you again—are you sure you can live with this? Are you sure? Are you sure?!"

I was in the living room, busily working on various prototype items. Megumin was in the living room, too, busily getting in my face with questions.

I was trying to develop a new product based on blending the sap of the tar plant with extract of Slime. Mix them together and you got a sort of half-dry vinyl.

I didn't stop working as I replied, "And I tell you again, Darkness is being too stubborn for me to do anything. We still have a whole week. If she comes crying back, I'll do something. And if she doesn't, I'll let it go."

As I spoke, I used a dropper to inject a burst of air into the vinyl-like substance. This stuff wasn't easy to manufacture. There had to be some way to mass-produce it, but at the prototype stage, I would just have to suck it up and do it by hand.

Aqua was lounging on the sofa nearby, humming to her egg, completely ignoring Megumin and me. It was about the most annoying thing I could think of, but it was still better than having her get in the way while I tried to do delicate R&D.

For some reason, it makes me sort of angry to realize she's actually a pretty good singer…

That was when Megumin grabbed my prototype. "Don't waste your time with this; think of a plan! I refuse to let you do this! If you sit around until the day of the wedding arrives, let me just say I have a few ideas of my own!"

She started to squeeze my prototype.

"Hey, don't cause a fuss, okay? You could make things worse for Darkness if you pull some dumb trick. In fact, she specifically asked me to keep you and Aqua from doing anything stupid. Come on, give that back. I've spent all day on it." I held out a hand in a *gimme* gesture.

"What is this anyway?" Megumin asked, inspecting the thing in her hand.

"I'm trying to re-create something we had in my country. It was called Bubble Wrap. I don't have the right materials or manufacturing processes, so it's not exactly the same, but I'm pretty pleased with my progress."

"What's it for?" Megumin said.

"You crush it, and it goes *pop-pop*. It's kind of a game. It makes you feel better."

"…………That's it?"

"That's it."

…………

Megumin gave my Bubble Wrap a great squeeze like she was ringing out a dishrag.

"Yaaaaah!"

"Aaaaaah?!"

Megumin let out a contented breath and tossed the ruined Bubble Wrap at me. "You're right. I do feel better," she said. "That was rather pleasant." Then she pattered outside, and I slumped to my knees.

A-all that work…!

Beside me, Aqua kept singing, as though the entire commotion had just passed her by.

"Stiiir, stiiir the se-sa-me mi-so, stiiir…"

"Pipe down already!" I spat at her. I didn't mean to, and it only made me hate myself.

……Damn it all!

There was no call to be mean to Aqua. What was I so upset about anyway?!

2

Six days until Darkness's wedding.

"A thousand pardons, but is Mr. Kazuma Satou here?" A butler in the first flush of old age was standing at the door of the mansion, where I had locked myself away.

"If you'll excuse my asking, who are you?" I said. But then I added, "Wait… Haven't I seen you before?"

That's right. I know this guy. He's a servant at Darkness's house.

"Yes, sir, and may I say it's a pleasure to see you again. My name is Hagen, head butler at the Dustiness household. I've come to beg you for your advice, Mr. Satou."

My advice? Had Darkness finally caved? Was she going to ask me for my help?

But of course, that was too much to hope for. Hagen, head bowed, held out an envelope. "Er, truth be told, letters such as this one have been arriving at the household on a daily basis…"

"Sorry! I'm very sorry. I'll take that idiot to task, believe me."

"N-not at all, sir. But I'm rather concerned she may escalate this and start sending them to Lord Alderp himself, which would be no small problem. I wanted to confer with you before that happened."

I crumpled the letter in my hand and threw myself apologetically to the ground in front of Hagen. I saw him off—apparently, this was all he'd wanted to say—and then glanced again at the letter in my hand.

To House Dustiness:

I have it on good authority that a general of the Demon King is threatening a terrorist attack against the Eris Church in Axel. The intended date of the attack is the day of the ceremony. If you do not call off the wedding immediately, this general will blow up the church. I implore you to take this warning seriously.

Signed,

A concerned mage

"Megumiiiin! I need to talk to you! Open up!" I shouted through the door of her room.

Four days until Darkness's wedding.

"All right! For my next trick, I'm going to pull a huge Beginner's Bane out of this tiny bag!"

"What are you talking about?! Don't pull out a man-eating monster! What are you doing? Come here!"

I grabbed Aqua, who was standing in the middle of a crowd smack in front of the Dustiness mansion.

"Hey, what do you think you're doing, Kazuma? Let me go! I posted a quest at the Adventurers Guild to get this Bane! And just look at how many people are here for a look at my amazing tricks!"

"I told you, the family summoned me here to stop you because you were making a scene right outside their house! What are you doing out here anyway?!"

Aqua was surrounded by curious onlookers, some of them tossing her the occasional coin.

"Oh, no tips, please," Aqua said. "I'm not a street entertainer, and

I can't accept them." She turned back to me and whispered, "Kazuma, this is all part of my plan for getting Darkness to come out of the house!"

Wait, is she…?

"You're doing these dumb tricks here hoping Darkness will notice you?"

"Exactly! Don't tell me you don't know the story of the Celestial Cave. The goddess Amaterasu hid herself away in the cave in anger, so the other gods held a big, noisy party just outside. When she came out to see what all the fuss was about, they blocked the cave so she couldn't go back in!"

"Of course I know that story. Is partying something gods like in every world? Please tell me all goddesses aren't like you."

Aqua ignored my jab, gesturing at the mansion with her bag. "The curtain in that room has been rustling all day. I just know it's Darkness, trying to sneak peeks to find out what's going on. Heeey! Darkness, I know you can hear me! Come on out, now! Believe me, you'll want to see the next one up close! I'm going to do my specialest, most amazing trick! …Hey, Kazuma, what are you doing? Let go!"

"I told you, they came to the mansion begging me to stop you. Come on, we're going home!"

"Uh-uh! I'm going to be here every day until I see Darkness! Leave me alone! Get out of here! Go on, get!"

Aqua showed no interest in listening to me. By the time I had dragged her back to the house, the sun was setting.

Two days until Darkness's wedding.

"I'm back…"

"Welcome home. You aren't going to do anything else stupid, are you?"

Megumin walked through the front door, but then stood dumbly in the foyer. She had ignored my lecture, sent one of her little threats to Lord Alderp, and consequently spent the last several days in jail.

"Darkness's family interceded for me and got me an early release…"

"So you set out to rescue her but ended up being rescued? That's pathetic. I understand how you feel, but just be an adult about this, all right? You and Aqua both are just causing trouble for them at this point."

Once again, I was trying my hand at a new product, but I took a break long enough to drive the point home with Megumin. Aqua, for her part, appeared to have gone to Darkness's house again today. Some vendors had set up shop out front, and the place had become a minor tourist attraction.

"I admit that it seems Aqua and I can do nothing on our own. Kazuma, will you at least help us crash this wedding?"

Megumin settled on the sofa, but apparently she wasn't done trying to convince me to get involved. After a moment, I said, "If Darkness comes and asks for help."

That caused Megumin to jump up again. "You faithless creature! They may call you Cad-zuma and Kaz-scum-ma around town, but I still saw you as someone who came through when it counted—and especially as someone who would never abandon a friend in need!"

I was still trying to work on my new item. "Hey, tell me who calls me that. I'd like to go straighten them out."

Megumin collapsed back on the sofa.

"At a time like this, the person I love might whine and complain at first, but he would ultimately say, *Well, nothing to it but to do it* and then figure something out, no matter what. That's just the kind of person he is. He is definitely not someone who just sits and sulks forever!"

"Wh-whatever. Don't think you can get me to help you just by suddenly being all, *I love you*. I'm not that soft."

The truth was, her words had caused my heart rate to spike. To cover for myself, and to try to placate Megumin, I pointed to the object I was working on.

"Instead of getting prickly, how about you try this out?" I suggested. "This is called a sandbag. It helps get rid of stress. And this one's real leather. It was kind of the only material that seemed suitable."

I pointed to the stress ball, a sewn leather pouch filled with sand, big enough to sit on the floor.

The idea of a stress buster seemed to get Megumin's attention. "How do you use it?" she asked.

"It's simple. Just attack it. You can punch it, kick it. Magic's off-limits, though, all right? I assume that goes without saying." I tried to sound joking as I left off my work and went to get some nice relaxing tea…

"Nnnggrraahhhhh!"

"Huh?!"

I whipped around at the sound of Megumin's shout, a very bad feeling in the pit of my stomach.

"Hmm. Yes, I do feel a bit relieved. If you don't mind, could you make another one for me?"

"Why would you use a sword?! I said punch or kick it!"

Megumin was holding my katana. She stood over my stress ball, now a sandy pile of garbage, looking just a tiny bit pleased with herself.

3

I had been experimenting with new products to pass the time until Darkness showed up. I had been so sure she would.

And yet here we were: Darkness's wedding day. We had arrived at the day of her matrimony, and Darkness had never come back to us.

"Kazuma, let's go! Let's go and ruin that ceremony! Heh-heh-heh! How easily a little magic can go awry and destroy a wedding hall—or a lord's mansion!"

"Hey, stop that. Seriously. It would be bad enough if we wound up back in debt, but they'd throw you in jail for real this time." I was organizing the items I wanted to show Vanir on the table in the living area. I had been hard at work coming up with new stuff, and I was almost done.

I mean really done. I couldn't think of one more idea. I had come up with blueprints of every possibility I could imagine for the efficient production of these items. Farming and stuff, too. I was no specialist, but I had the same basic familiarity as any Japanese person would, and I had written down everything I could think of.

The wedding ceremony was supposed to be that afternoon, but I had no intention of attending. If she wasn't going to come ask me for help, then I sure wasn't going to stick my neck out.

It was just stupid, stubborn pride. I knew that, and yet…

Megumin looked at me, clutching her staff with a distraught look on her face. Her voice grew harsh as she said, "The person I love is not someone who would remain so awful and unfeeling forever! Kazuma! How can you bear to know that Darkness is going to be married to that lord?! Can you abide the thought of him having his way with her?!"

"Of course I can't!" I found myself shouting back at her.

My unexpected reaction set Megumin back on her heels.

"Of course I can't," I repeated. "I hate the thought of letting him take her away! He isn't just ugly—everyone knows he's a terrible person! You may not know it, but I've heard that he'll do anything and everything to get his hands on whatever cute thing catches his eye. And when he's tired of her, he just gives her a little bit of cash and then dumps her. He's awful, and he does all these awful things, but for some reason no one has ever been able to prove it!"

Megumin stood there looking at the ground and sniffling as she absorbed all this.

"Sorry," I said. "I decided to investigate this guy she was getting married to…"

When I did, I found out the guy in question was even worse than rumor told. I'm no private eye, and even I was able to dig up an endless supply of terrible stories about him. Exploitation, bribery—the list went on and on. Yet, strangely, there was never any physical proof. The women he victimized were forcibly silenced, and supposedly he had enough people in his pocket, even at the national level, to keep evidence of his deeds from ever getting out.

Darkness's dad had been sent here, apparently, to find that evidence and to keep an eye on Alderp.

Megumin's grip on her staff tightened. "Then that's all the more reason we can't let this go on, isn't it? Kazuma, surely you have some dirty trick in mind? Surely this will be just as it's always been—Aqua and I have tried and failed, but now you'll step up and succeed. Won't you?"

Dirty trick? Who did she think I was?

"This time, Megumin... This time, I can't do anything. For starters, Darkness wouldn't tell me how much the debt was. Next, even if I could come up with the money, I wouldn't be able to convince Darkness to accept it. She's too stubborn; she'd never take it. And finally..."

Megumin cocked her head. "Yes? Finally what?"

"This is a marriage between noble houses. Security's going to be tight. I don't think we could get close if we wanted to. Honestly, that's part of why I've been waiting for Darkness to come to us. I'm sure they upped the guard at the Dustiness mansion after I broke in. I don't think I could get in there a second time."

I had never paid much attention to the social difference between us, but then, it had never hurt this much before. Megumin stood silently, watching me. I turned my back to her, unable to meet her gaze any longer. I probably looked like some guy who was sulking about having his girl stolen from him...

"Darkness's dad is really sick. I don't think they would let us see him if we asked. And I don't have any noble connections I could use to score an invitation to the wedding... I'm just a commoner, after all."

I had thought of the friends I made in the capital, and maybe I could have leaned on Iris—but if Darkness and Alderp both wanted this marriage to go ahead, then there really wasn't anything to be done.

A difference in social position. That's all this was. The simple fact that we had been able to go adventuring with Darkness for so long, despite inhabiting such different worlds, was a miracle in itself.

I informed Megumin of all this as offhandedly as I could.

"I understand," she said. "Knowing that you investigated the other party, that you did try to do something, is enough for me." As hard as I was trying not to look at her, she managed to gaze into my eyes. She smiled; she seemed somehow at peace. "I will think of something myself and travel a path that will leave me without regret. Kazuma… I hope you'll do the same."

What had she had in her breakfast that morning? She sounded so serious. And…wise. Almost like an honest-to-goodness mage.

I sat, slightly openmouthed, as Megumin pattered out of the mansion.

Should I stop her?

It doesn't matter… I could stop her, but we can't stop this wedding.

I watched Megumin leave, and then I was all alone in the living room. It suddenly felt huge.

Aqua, oddly enough, had a visitor. Right then they were talking in her room on the second floor. It sounded like some kind of urgent business, but today of all days, I just couldn't work myself up to help Aqua with whatever it was.

This was the room where we all got together and lazed around when we didn't have anything better to do. Being there by myself made me realize how big this house was, and how lonely.

There's nothing I can do…

Going adventuring with the daughter of a noble family? Back in Japan, I could never have imagined it.

Reality was never so convenient.

I sank into the sofa and heaved a sigh.

A violent slam from the front door popped the bubble of my melancholy. And who should be standing there but—?

"Good day to you all! The all-seeing demon has come to your collective aid, excepting your miserable excuse for a goddess. You would do well to weep and dance with joy at my arrival. Now then, show me the many fruits of your knowledge!"

4

"Go away! Bring me that beautiful shopkeeper instead! I wanna trade! Why do I have to talk business with you when I'm so stressed? I wish I could change you into that beautiful shopkeeper! Wiz! I want Wiz!"

Vanir simply sat down at the living room table across from me. "Your pretty little friend is presently working the floor, although she is weeping all the while that she wanted to sleep in a little more. It's had a surprising effect. People find a tearful shopkeeper adorable, or they think she's shedding tears of joy from the sheer pleasure of salesmanship and buy more to indulge her. Anyway, do you honestly think that debt machine could hold a decent business meeting? Yesterday, when I relaxed enough to give her some time off—well, I took my eyes off her for one second, and when I looked back, she had ordered this pendant. 'Adventuring couples will love it!' she says!"

He showed me a piece of jewelry.

"And what does the pendant do?" I asked.

"When the person wearing it is on the edge of death, the pendant utilizes their last breath of life to explode. 'Protect your loved ones to the bitter end,' that's the idea. Very romantic, isn't it? That's what *she* thinks anyway. But the power of the explosion would blow away your loved ones along with your enemies. It makes me doubt whether she has any sense for business at all. Want to buy one?"

"I-I'll pass, thanks. So what's this about you coming here to help us?"

Vanir, however, said, "We will come to that later. First, bring out your prospective wares. My all-seeing eye shall quickly discern which are viable. Although—ahem—I've taken the liberty of bringing with me a sum of money that I don't think you'll refuse."

He placed a small black bag on the table with a heavy *thump*. Being all-seeing certainly did make one more efficient.

"Hey now, you can't be sure I'll accept," I said. "This stuff represents all the ideas I had left after last time. I'm not going to let them go for cheap, you know."

And if it couldn't help me to help Darkness, then there was no point in selling anyway.

Vanir, as if to emphasize his omniscience, said, "O young man who so wishes to go help the armored girl but fears being rejected by her if he does so. I, the all-seeing demon Vanir, hereby declare: You will desire to take the contents of this bag in exchange for your intellectual property rights to all these items."

Man…having an all-seeing demon around was no joke.

Vanir hardly looked at my blueprints and prototypes, let alone the intellectual property contracts, as he stuffed them all into a giant bag. I guess he probably didn't need to look at them.

Hang on. I didn't say I would sell yet…

Oh yeah… All-seeing demon.

"Hey, Vanir… You know a lot of stuff, right?" I tried to sound nonchalant, as if we were going to discuss the weather.

Vanir didn't look at me but continued stuffing paperwork into his bag. "Mm, indeed. Not precisely all things, but a great many. For example, I know of course what you intend to ask next. Why, you want to know, is the armored girl's family in such crushing debt to that lord? Is there no way to help her? Why has there never been any proof despite all the crimes that lord has committed?"

I swallowed hard.

"Tell me… Why are you—?"

"Helping you despite being a demon? You wonder if I'm planning something and so on and so forth. Of course I am. I *am* a demon, after all. But in this particular case, my interests align with yours. Hence why I'm so helpful. Perhaps, for example, I will ask you to sell to me your seemingly quite valuable intellectual property rights at a deep discount." He closed his bag and smirked at me.

Grr. What a jerk…

"But if I say I won't sell, then it's game over, isn't it? If the answers to my questions are so obvious to you, then why don't you just come out and tell me?"

"Good! Very well. I shall inform you, then, of what you wish to know! The color and pattern of the underwear the shopkeeper is wearing today are— Hmm? What's this? I sense none of your usual delicious negativity."

"Because I do want to know that, but later."

"I—I see. In that case, I shall inform you of what you *truly* wish to know! The reason that girl is in debt is—"

"*Sacred Exorcism*!"

Aqua's spell interrupted Vanir before he could finish, surrounding him in a pillar of light. When it finally faded, there was a clatter as Vanir's mask fell to the ground.

"No! Vanir! You're a big-deal demon, right?! Speak to me! You can't be finished just because the goddess of toilets attacked you! Come on, man, come on!"

"Ahhh! Kazuma! I take my eyes off you for one second, and you go and get brainwashed by a demon? Why are you acting like he's your friend?! And I'm the goddess of *water*!"

Aqua had spotted Vanir as she was coming down from the second floor and had let fly with her magic. She was still poised to cast as she shouted at me. She really had just the worst possible timing!

Behind her stood a man in early old age—a man I recognized. It was Darkness's butler, who had shown up here to complain on an almost daily basis. I didn't know what he had been asking Aqua for, but now the man—Hagen was his name—stood blinking in surprise.

As we watched, Vanir's mask rose up into the air, supported by a body that grew out of nothing.

Awfully convenient how it came with clothes and everything… Or maybe the clothes were actually part of his body? That would explain why they were destroyed by Aqua's magic.

"Bwa-ha-ha-ha-ha. A surprise attack? Nice try—are you a goddess or a street goon? I think there's more demon in you than you would like to admit! Behold: A crack has appeared in my awesome mask!"

"Ewww! I have nothing to do with demons! Don't you pretend I have anything to do with demons! If you expect me to ask for permission every time I crush a bug or exorcise a demon, you're going to be disappointed. How stupid can you be? Pfft, hee-hee-hee!"

The staring contest between the two supernaturals was looking more and more dangerous, so I hurriedly jumped in. "Okay, all right, save it! Aqua, I really want to hear what Vanir is saying right now, so butt out!"

She backed down a little at that. Hagen seemed to sense the dangerous mood and said, "I-it appears you're in the middle of something. I'll show myself out. Lady Arch-priest, we're scheduled to begin at noon, remember. I'll see you shortly…"

He slipped between Aqua and Vanir, making himself as small as possible, and darted out the door. I was curious what exactly he had wanted from Aqua, but right now, Vanir was more important.

The demon looked at Aqua, and the corners of his mouth turned up triumphantly. "Bwa-ha-ha-ha! O impotent goddess who is unable to be of any help in this instance! See now how useful and worthy of gratitude I am and tear up a handkerchief or something in frustration!"

Then he stuck out his tongue at her. I guess being a demon didn't necessarily make you a grown-up.

Aqua's eyebrows shot up, but we were in danger of this conversation never getting anywhere. Aqua came over and sat in between where I was on the sofa and where Vanir was on the other side of the table, clutching her egg protectively. Maybe she just wanted to listen in on our conversation, but in fact she was sitting practically nose to nose with Vanir, staring him down.

"I'm finding this highly difficult," Vanir said. "But all the same. Young man who fails to petition the gods in prayer even though a goddess is living in his own house. It's the story of that armored girl's debt that you're interested in, isn't it? It began back when you adventurers vanquished Mobile Fortress Destroyer." He sounded as relaxed as if he were discussing his plans for the afternoon.

……………………

What did he just say?

"Hey. Details."

Vanir smiled at that. He didn't bother to act self-important but went on easily. "Details? You know Destroyer trampled over all the other towns it encountered. Those lords lost their domains. The populace was out of house and home, and without any land to their names, those lords were relieved of their governing responsibilities—as well as their noble titles. Each and every one of them wound up wandering the streets. For you no-account adventurers, it might even have been the better outcome. But regardless, in your case, it was not to be."

But that's…good, isn't it?

Vanir smiled as if he could read this thought, too. "Yes, your town was saved. Those who work here suffered nothing, nor did most of those who live here. And the Mobile Fortress itself collapsed just outside the city. *That* led to a good deal of destruction, including of the grain-producing areas immediately nearby and the flood works within them."

…Well, sure. But we had kept the damage to a minimum, hadn't we?

"Those who relied on farming for their livelihood, in effect, lost their business and all their assets. A devastated field doesn't grow back overnight. So they went to the local lord for help."

…I didn't like where this was going. I frowned.

"Precisely—it is exactly as you imagine! The lord said to them, 'Don't be ridiculous. Isn't it enough to have escaped with your lives? If you want to complain, complain to the adventurers who couldn't protect your fields. They're swimming in cash from their reward right now. Go claim a bit of it for yourselves…'"

…Yikes. How much more of a stereotypical villain could you be?

"Indeed. It may be that there is no blame in this case besides that of the greedy governor who abandoned his responsibilities. You adventurers performed above and beyond the call of duty; there's no question of that. But that didn't change anything for the handful of victims. They still had nowhere to go. Can you blame them for being upset? What would you tell them? That this was akin to an act of God, and they should forget about it? Hardly."

Vanir gave a truly demonic smirk.

Then he said something I couldn't ignore—and he said it as casually as if it was nothing at all.

"The aggrieved citizens went crying to… Yes, you guessed it. Your dear Dustinesses! 'Oh, Dustiness family!' they said. 'When some pitiful adventurers destroyed the town with a flood, you paid for the vast majority of the reconstruction. Now we ask you to find it in your hearts to have mercy on us as well…'"

……

"Wait just a second. What did you say? What was that about destroying the town with a flood?"

Now Vanir seemed to be getting proper demonic enjoyment out of this conversation.

"Did you really think a few hundred million eris would cover destruction of that magnitude? Perhaps you recall that when the Guild asked you for restitution, they requested you pay 'at least a part' of the full amount."

That *woman*!

"The Dustinesses put the vast majority of their assets, with the exception of their mansion, into paying for the damaged buildings. And when Destroyer happened, the heavily armored daughter of the family saw that her house was now without any resources yet still wished to help the needy townspeople. And so she went to that very lord, the one who had shirked his duty, and begged him to let her borrow money."

That *woman*, doing all that without even asking anyone!

"He was disinclined to help but agreed to lend the funds on the condition that if anything should happen to the head of the Dustiness family and his repayment be imperiled, guarantee would be made in the form of 'her body'—"

Vanir was interrupted by the sound of my fist hitting the table. Aqua flinched. I stuck my hand out at her.

"Hey… Hey, Kazuma, that must have hurt when you hit the table all angry like that. It hurt, didn't it?"

Now it all made sense. That jerk butler who had come to the house must have been a messenger from Alderp. He knew that Darkness's dad was in ill health, and he was demanding repayment of the debt. Darkness had come up with the ridiculous idea of defeating the hydra in order to earn the money. But then she saw all the adventurers I had gotten together to help her and decided she couldn't worry us with this problem anymore…

"And how much is Darkness's debt?" I asked Vanir quietly.

I guess Vanir had expected even that question, because he simply took the bag he had brought and slid it toward me. "Exactly as much as your own holdings plus what's in this bag. Now, shall we talk business?"

Dammit! He's a demon, all right!

5

"Beautiful! You're so beautiful, milady! After the ceremony, you must go to your honored father's room so he can see you!"

The new maid smiled with pleasure to see me in my dress.

A pained grin was the only reply I could manage. This girl was new to our house; she didn't know our family history, and she didn't know the story of this wedding. If I were to let Father see me like this, it could only bring him sadness.

I knew full well that this wedding would make no one happy. This was about my own self-satisfaction.

There was a commotion from the hallway. I could hear someone shouting on the other side of the door.

"What do you mean, I can't see the bride?! Out of my way! I can't wait! I can't wait any longer! Lalatina will be mine in just a matter of hours! Now or later, who cares? Move, I told you! Lalatina! Lalatinaaaa!"

...Heh. So he was done pretending to be a decent human being.

A member of my family's staff replied as gently as he could, "Sir, you mustn't. This is the waiting room of House Dustiness. And until the ceremony is over, only members of the Dustiness family may enter. Please, sir, step back."

"You damnable fools! Know this: When this ceremony is over, *I* will be your master. Let that sink in for a moment, and then decide whether or not you want to let me through that door."

The man didn't sound flustered by this outrageous statement. "I cannot let you through, sir. You are not my master."

After a moment, the cruel voice replied, "...Don't think I'll forget this. After the wedding—and after I've enjoyed your precious *young lady* to my heart's content—I'll deal with you. Just you wait."

Then I heard my husband-to-be stomping away.

"...Could you call the man by the door?" I said. "I'd like to thank him."

The maid nodded quietly and summoned the staff member posted outside.

"Young Lady! How truly lovely you look..." He sounded at once overjoyed and just a little bit sad.

He was one of the guards who had been in the service of our house for a very long time. He was not one to bend; I remembered being a child and begging him to let me out of the house, but he never gave in. I would try to sneak over the fence, but he would always find me out.

At one point in my life, I entertained elaborate fantasies of outfoxing him and escaping. Once, I tossed a ball over the fence and then begged him to go get it for me. While he was off fetching it, I snuck out. He found me almost immediately and dragged me back home—but I enjoyed the experience so much that I started throwing a ball over the fence every day. Every day, he would let me convince him to go get it. Looking back on it now, I realize that this was just after my mother died and I had no one to play with; in his own way, this man was being a playmate for me.

"I'm sorry about that...," I said. "You could have let him through. It doesn't matter what happens to me now. But rest assured, I'll guarantee he doesn't punish you."

"You need not worry, Young Lady," the guard said. "It was my intention to resign after your marriage in any event. I serve House Dustiness—although I could be moved to serve a man who had won your respect."

I gave him a sad smile. A man who had won my respect? An image flitted through my mind: a certain boy who had snuck into my room at night, been chased off, offered a parting shot as he jumped out a window, and then lay rolling on the ground in pain. I couldn't keep the corners of my lips from creeping up at the memory.

"Your smile is so beautiful, Miss, but all too rare these days. It warms my heart to have seen that expression on my last day of service to you." The guard gave me a beatific smile of his own, then turned away. "...A-ahem. If I may be so forward, the beauty of your innocence is your loveliest trait. Er...so...perhaps you could satisfy yourself without letting your little games become too violent..." With these embarrassed words, he vanished to the other side of the door.

"?!"

The two maids both averted their gazes. Ohhh! What I wouldn't give to get my hands on the guy who started these awful rumors with his impressions!

He's foul-mouthed, rude, and totally lacks what you would assume to be common knowledge despite a head full of obscure trivia. He's conservative and a coward, yet given to sudden bursts of outrageous behavior; he just doesn't make sense. He's of the weakest class, has totally average stats besides his Luck, and has managed to defeat generals of the Demon King, major bounty heads, and every kind of monster using nothing but his plethora of skills and a little opportunism. He's a mystery. When I revealed to him that I was a noble, he was less interested in my status than he was amused by my name.

And then…

I was the one who offered to cross the uncrossable line with him. I must be one messed-up person.

I thought back on all our adventures, all the fun times we had. It's very unusual for a noble to ever get to follow her own heart, including in the matter of marriage. And yet I had been permitted to spend my entire life up to this point with my own friends, doing what I wanted.

…That was enough. It would be greedy for a noble like me to hope for any more. Now it was my turn to repay the people of this town. No longer would I let that lord do whatever he wanted. While he was busying himself with my body, I would learn his secrets. It might take years, but with the memory of my friends to sustain me, I could endure.

…It was the strangest thing, though: I once thought it wouldn't be half-bad to be his wife, but now I felt no attraction to him at all. Was this all *his* fault, too? Every time I thought back to our fights, I found myself starting to smile.

"Er, Y-Young Lady?" My sudden smile had confused the maid who was doing my makeup; she stopped her work.

"Oh. Pardon me. It's nothing."

I told her to keep working, and then I let my thoughts wander back to my friends and their quirks.

What would they do if they knew why I was in debt? Megumin would probably get angry. Aqua might start to cry even though she didn't understand what was going on.

And him? He would maybe say, *How could you do something so stupid?!* Then he would find out the thing that annoyed me most and immediately do it.

But after I found out that lord's secrets and put an end to all this… Would my friends still accept me? Would they take me back?

"You look brilliant, milady! Please, if you'll come to the mirror..."

I obediently followed the maid to the looking glass, where I saw myself in a white dress. I gave myself the faintest of smiles. What a disappointment that I was doing all this dressing up for that lord.

The ceremony was closed to the common people, but outside the church at the reception, anyone and everyone would be able to see me. Would *he* be there?

...No. No, of course not. I knew him. I was sure he was shut up in his room alone, sulking. The thought of him pouting made me smile again.

"It's time. Let's go, milady. The priest who will be officiating this most joyous occasion is the most powerful cleric in all of Axel. You'll have the most wonderful wedding ceremony, I'm sure..."

The man saying these words, ushering me out with a gesture, was none other than my family's longest-serving butler, Hagen.

I made to go, grateful to this town and all the people who had given me such freedom until this day.

Ah... It's been fun.

Every day of the last year had been a joy.

The smallest of smiles crept over my lips, and I took Hagen's outstretched hand...

6

This was the holiest place in all of Axel.

The center of the cult of Axis and their crazy— Er, obviously not.

Naturally, we were in the Eris Church building.

Most of those in attendance were people of power and influence in the town or nobles from nearby areas. All of them knew this wedding was a farce. They chatted in their seats, with none of the anxious anticipation that usually accompanies a wedding ceremony about to start.

Guards serving "that lord" were posted outside the church, holding back the hangers-on who were trying to get a glimpse of the bride. The majority of said hangers-on were adventurers. Since Darkness's marriage had recently become public knowledge, they were probably trying to see what their usually armor-clad acquaintance looked like in a dress. They were going nuts trying to get a peek. Well, maybe curiosity was what had driven them to become adventurers in the first place.

Finally, the buzz died down, and silence descended over the church.

Two small rooms had been prepared to the left and right of the building's entrance, one for the groom and one for the bride.

Now, out of the bride's room, Hagen led the wife-to-be in a brilliant white dress. The butler was probably there as a fill-in for Darkness's father, who was too sick to attend. A veil hid Darkness's face, yet even so, she possessed a beauty that captivated onlookers.

Next, the lord appeared from the other room. A white tuxedo hugged his corpulent frame, and like everyone else in the church, he couldn't take his eyes off Darkness. No, he couldn't take his eyes off her, his mouth hanging half-open, staring stupidly…

He started to drift toward her, but Hagen gave a discreet cough, and the lord came to his senses. But it was almost as if no one noticed his pathetic behavior, because they were all too fixated on the bride.

At last, the church's pipe organ struck up a dignified march, and the bride and groom began walking down the aisle together. The groom didn't have his eyes on where he was going but was looking entirely at Darkness.

Darkness, for her part, never looked up but kept her eyes on the ground. Seeing her like that, I felt a tremendous rage well up in me.

"Do you think he might starve me? Refuse to give me food or water? It's enough to make my heart pound…!" Whatever!

What happened to the pervert I knew? The one who would blush at the thought of the monsters we were fighting? The one who could make impromptu declarations that brought even a general of the Demon King up short?

This was her wedding, yet Darkness didn't look the least bit happy. She looked sad, lonely. At long last, all eyes still on her, she arrived at the altar, where they would exchange their vows.

Right in front of me.

That's right: I was standing beside the altar.

In this world, it seemed, any cleric could administer wedding vows. You didn't have to follow a specific religion. Say, for example, that you were the only Arch-priest in a whole town full of novices.

The person Hagen had asked to do the blessing of the vows, the person who was now standing smack at the center of the altar, was the Arch-priest—and therefore most highly ranked cleric in Axel—Lady Aqua herself.

And me? I stood proudly beside her as her assistant.

Even when they arrived at the front of the church, the groom was too busy looking at his soon-to-be wife to notice us, and the blushing bride continued to stare at the ground.

The solemn march stopped, and a voice began speaking. But it wasn't half as reverent as the music that had just been playing.

"Darkness. You are here today to marry this man who appears to be the offspring of a bear and a pig, in contravention of orders from me, a goddess, and allowed yourself to be swept along by events. Do you swear to take this old fart in sickness and in health, in happiness and in sadness, for richer or for poorer? Do you swear to love this old fart, respect him, *comfort* and help him, and to protect your chastity with your life? You can't do it, can you? I'd sure like to just go home with you, Darkness. We could pick at Kazuma's cooking and toss back a drink..."

Wait, that wasn't how wedding vows went, was it? The attention of everyone in the church instantly switched to Aqua. Even Alderp managed to bring himself to look at her.

"…?! What? I—I know you! You're that woman who showed up at my house and caused me all kinds of trouble! What is this? What in the world are you doing here?!"

His shouting caused Darkness to notice us at last, and she stared at us, her mouth working open and closed with shock.

I took the opportunity to grab her by the arm.

Mom, Dad?

I know you did your best to raise a normal child. But your beloved son has given up any hope of a normal life and is about to pick a fight with the biggest fish around. He's going to kidnap a noblewoman.

Darkness went pale as she registered what was happening, tears springing to her eyes.

"Wh-what *is* this? Aqua… K-Kazuma! Kazuma, let go! Let go of me! What in Eris's name do you think you're doing?! This isn't fun and games anymore! Crashing a noble wedding ceremony? You'll be lucky if execution is the worst you get! How could you be so stupid? How could you be so, so stupid?"

I didn't let her get carried away any further.

"Shut it, you moron! Running off on your own to play some idiot game! Deciding to take on my debt without so much as a word to me! Who do you think you are, my wife?! I told you—if you love me, you should have said something!"

"That's the dumbest thing I've ever heard! I'm sure I don't have the slightest idea what you're talking about, you big idiot!"

So maybe a church wasn't the best place for this argument, but we didn't care. The would-be groom, however, finally collected himself.

"Th-the boy! Arrest the boy! And that fraud of a priest! They're peasants! Commoners! They don't belong here! Arrest them!"

He tried to grab Darkness back from me, but I gave her a tug and hid her behind my back. *That* made Alderp angry.

"Blast it all! You've got nothing to do with this—so butt out! Your beloved Lalatina owes me a debt, one so large that a worthless creature like you couldn't repay it if you slaved your entire life! If you want your woman back, go save up your allowance and then talk to me—as if you have a chance!"

The opportunity was just too perfect. I picked up the bag I had set beside the altar.

"I'll take that offer, old man," I said. "Get a load of this: two billion eris, Darkness's entire debt! Two thousand magic silver coins worth a million eris each. So I'll be taking Darkness, thank you! And just for the record, she's not my beloved! She's j-just my friend! A very important friend—but just a friend!"

My diligent corrections were almost drowned out by the clatter as I dumped all two thousand coins right at Alderp's feet.

And why would I do that, you ask…?

"Whaaa—?! What do you mean, two billion?! Argh, wait! Lalatina! My Lalatina! Ahh—my money! Quickly, pick that up!"

He started scrambling to grab the cash—as did everyone else in attendance. Hey, it wasn't my fault if some unscrupulous bystander picked up some of the coins.

While they were all busy with that, I took Darkness by the hand—she showed no sign of moving on her own—and tried to get away from the advancing group of what appeared to be Alderp's goons.

Darkness, though, shoved my hand away and shouted, "How—how could you?! Nobody asked you to do this! Do you have no respect for my personal resolve?! And this money! Where in the whole wide world did you come up with this much money?!" Darkness had been so stalwart until this moment, but now she was truly upset.

"I did some selling," I said. "Specifically, I sold all my knowledge of and rights to any idea I might ever have, in perpetuity. The money I got from doing that, plus every speck of reward money I'd saved up, came to exactly two billion eris. So I'm back to having to do honest work. I already made the sale. No use crying over it. I can't go back on the deal now. Get it? So let's go!"

Darkness looked at me with a flurry of emotions—astonishment, sadness, and joy. But apparently she still had more to say.

"You did all *that*? You— How could you—? When I— We—?"

Alderp's guys were rushing at us, and I was out of patience. I grabbed Darkness by the shoulders and shook her as hard as I could. "Cut the chitchat already! You don't have any right to say no, and I won't take any more back talk from you! I bought you back from that old-fart lord, so you're my property now! I'm going to work you like a dog, and don't you forget it! Get ready, because you're gonna use that body of yours to recover everything I spent on you, you perverted, masochistic Crusader! You got that?! If you get it, then lemme hear it!!"

"Y-yesh, shirrr!"

The shaking, the shouting, and the being called a pervert in front of a whole crowd caused tears to spring to Darkness's eyes but also sent her into a sort of ecstatic trance; she answered me in a mesmerized slur.

I still had Darkness by the shoulders when she pitched forward. Apparently, my little speech had tugged on her heartstrings—or, more to the point, scored a critical hit on her hopeless masochism.

Why did I always end up having to drag her along at the most crucial moments?! I swept her up in my arms like I was rescuing a damsel in distress and made for the church door.

Now, remember, all kinds of noble and influential people from around town were attending this ceremony. The kinds of people who didn't deal well with crisis or with any sort of immediate physical danger. None of them tried to stop me; other than the crew grabbing money off the ground, they just watched me go.

Darkness, writhing in my arms, was blushing harder than I had ever seen her, and her breath was growing dangerously harsh.

"*Hff*… *Hff*… B-bought…! A noble like me, bought! By *this* man!

P-pay you back with my body? Unbelievable! And look—look at the situation we're in! Carried off from my own wedding like a captive princess, like a—like a—"

"H-hey, watch the drool! Watch out, you're drooling on me! You sure you're all right?! I mean, are you even *sane*?!"

For some reason, Aqua, making up the tail of our little train, seemed pleased about all this; her eyes were shining as she said, "Ah, Kazuma the cur strikes again! All Darkness did was take on your debt, and all you did was pay it back again, but you manage to act as if you've bought her! Hey, Kazuma, I think when Megumin hears about this pay-with-your-body business, she's gonna hit you with a major explosion. If she manages to totally vaporize you, I won't be able to bring you back, okay?"

"St-stop that! You need to stop making everything sound so bad! You're twisting my words! I meant she would have to use her body like, like work! As a Crusader! As an adventurer!"

Even as I spoke, I could see Alderp's men gathering in the aisle to block our exit. And my arms were still full with Darkness, who was still blushing and melting.

"Damn! Hey, Darkness, how long do you plan to keep up the crazy-in-love act? Get on your own two feet and start running! And by the way, all those muscles make you awfully heavy!"

"Y-you bastard! How could you spoil the mood by saying something like that?!" Darkness, tears in her eyes once again, tore the train off her dress so she could move more easily, then jumped out of my arms. "Well, we've come too far to stop now! I'm sick and tired of all this! You, Alderp's dogs! Get out of my way or die where you stand!"

Next, she lost the veil, her golden hair streaming behind her as she threw herself at the goons. They caught hold of her, trying to stop her; she didn't even attempt to dodge them but only stretched out her hands. Person after person grabbed her shoulders, her arms, but it didn't matter; she dragged them all along, and with each hand she reached out and grabbed the guys clinging to her by the face.

Ah, the ol' Iron Talon. The thugs could only make pathetic squeaking sounds.

"For crying out loud, we came all this way to rescue you, and you throw yourself right at them?! Aqua, back her up! Get on it, now!"

"Leave it to me! You want my entertainer magic, by any chance?"

"Just what the doctor ordered! I love that spell!"

Behind us, Alderp was still desperately sweeping up money, as were a few of the guests. Now equipped with Aqua's special spell, I covered my mouth and then shouted: "You lot! Forget about them—we'll deal with them another day. Get over here and help me collect my money!"

I was imitating Alderp's voice, naturally. It worked.

"Huh?" the thugs said, interrupting their duel with Darkness. "Y-yes, sir! Right away, sir!"

They rushed past us and over to where their lord was trying to claim his debt.

"You idiots!" he exclaimed. "Why are *you* over here?! Go bring back my Lalatina!"

"?!"

They came rushing back toward us. Now we had close to a dozen of them on both sides. Their arms and armor weren't anything noteworthy, but even with Aqua's buffs, it was an open question whether we would be able to push past them.

This was it. Time for me to get serious again, just like I'd done at the castle. I had stolen back my friend, and I was starting to feel pretty heroic. That was when—

"*Light of Saber*!!"

A familiar voice rang from the door, and a bright light carved through the bricks of the church wall.

This was a spell favored by the Crimson Magic Clan, one that allowed them to imbue a knife with light magic that could cut through anything.

After a moment, the door, and the entire wall around it, simply fell over. Bright daylight streamed in, silhouetting two figures. The adventurers who had been gathered around outside were giving them a wide berth, a nice, respectful distance… They also appeared to be very eager to see what would happen next.

"Megumin, I did it! I—I did it! Because we're friends, right? F-for a friend like you, I would do anything, even commit what's basically a crime, like this! I mean, you were all, 'I beg you to help me, my friend!' and how could I say no?"

"Yes, yes, fine work, Yunyun. That is my friend for you. You can go back to your inn now."

"Whaaat?!"

Two girls with crimson eyes stood before us. Megumin took a step forward, and that was enough to send the lord's servants scuttling back. Their collective gaze was fixed on the glowing tip of Megumin's staff.

Geez, look at this… It was obvious her reputation as the girl who wouldn't hesitate to blow up anything and everything in pursuit of her goals was now complete.

Megumin raised up her staff, looking more serious than I had ever seen her. The red of her eyes seemed to glow. She gave a dramatic flap of her cape.

That was when I heard a quiet murmur run through the assembled crowd.

"The evil wizard has come. The evil wizard is here to steal away the bride."

To be fair, I had stolen Darkness first. But standing there in the church entryway, framed by the sunlight, Megumin looked more heroic than I ever had.

…And this was supposed to be my moment!

7

Each person in the church, noble and goon alike, was watching every move of the "evil wizard" with an emotion akin to panic.

"You are all acquainted with my nickname, I presume? Then you must know what magic brims at the end of this staff. I warn you, it takes a great deal of focus to control this spell… If I were to be surprised and my concentration suddenly broken, it would be *bang*! Good-bye! If you have any intention of trying to stop me, do so with that in mind."

So basically, if anyone so much as tried to lay a hand on her, she would "lose control" and blow the place to smithereens.

Whoever the "evil wizard" was, they would be proud of this performance.

Alderp's people formed a circle around Megumin, but they didn't look very happy about it; they carefully kept their distance. All of them—the ones Darkness had charged at and the ones I had sent back in the other direction—seemed none too eager to get their hands on us.

Yunyun, standing beside Megumin, took a glance around the church.

"Wait…what? Look, Megumin, Mr. Kazuma is already here…"

Finally, Megumin noticed Aqua and me, along with Darkness in her torn dress. She seemed to grasp immediately what had happened, because a broad smile came over her face. Then she pointed her staff at us. She was giving us a way out: At the mere gesture, the goons in front of us scuttled away and hid among the pews.

The three of us took the opportunity to head for Megumin and Yunyun, but Alderp, *still* collecting his money, shouted: "Wh-what are you fools doing, letting her intimidate you? She's bluffing; she has to be! Who would use explosion magic in a place like this? It's obvious what would happen! Stop them!"

That, however, was all it took.

* * *

"Oh-ho! Intimidate? Bluff? Do you truly believe that I would ever mention explosion magic with anything less than total sincerity? Well! Very well! I accept your challenge!"

This sent our antagonists into a panic.

"Stop! We won't get anywhere near you, so please, stop!"

"We swear not to attack you, so please don't do it!"

"Lord Alderp! I beg you not to provoke her!"

Just how gruesome *was* her reputation? I mean, even Megumin wouldn't set off an explosion right in the middle of town.

...Would...she...?

With the goons shaking in their boots, the three of us managed to link up with Megumin and Yunyun.

"I was about to do something really cool!" I shouted. "And you had to go and steal the spotlight! But you did save our necks, so thanks."

Megumin laughed. "Crimson Magic Clan members have a sixth sense for dramatic opportunities. Given all your jabbering, Kazuma, I assumed you would do something eventually. But I admit I didn't expect you to show up here before I did!" She actually seemed a little bit pleased.

"Megumin! And Yunyun, they got you, too—? When we get home... We can talk when... I'll thank you after we—"

Maybe Darkness was overwhelmed with gratitude, or maybe the excitement of earlier hadn't quite worn off. Whatever the case, she seemed unable to produce an entire sentence.

"Why so distant?" Megumin said, almost a little shy. "We're...party members, aren't we? Friends. Surely you didn't think we would let such a f-fine Crusader go so easily!" She seemed to hope her emphatic finish would conceal how awkward she felt about admitting her friendship.

"*Friends*," Yunyun breathed. "That has such a nice ring to it, Megumin! And if—if a dear personal acquaintance like me were to be in this same situation, you would have come to help me, right?"

"No. A close personal acquaintance you may be, but you're also my self-proclaimed rival… We aren't exactly friends in the way party members are."

"?!"

Gosh, and Yunyun was leaning into the friendship thing so much. You're merciless, Megumin.

"Hey, I'm sorry, but I don't think this is the time for cute banter!" Aqua interjected. "We need to do something about this!"

Alderp's lackeys were slowly encircling us where we stood at the entrance to the church. I didn't think they would attack us while Megumin was there; she was the most dangerous person in the room, and her notoriously short fuse was lit.

The local lord, however, had evidently had enough of his subordinates' reluctance. "All of you out there!" he shouted. "I can tell by the look of you that you're adventurers. These people are criminals! Take my bride back from them! A rich reward awaits her rescuer, I assure you. For starters, I'll hire you as a guard at my mansion! You need never grub about on another adventure again! Now, bring her to me! Bring me Lalatina!"

The onlooking adventurers, who had been watching all this develop with no small interest, now exchanged a collective look. Nobody moved. In fact, they spontaneously began to look in the other direction or yawn and pretend they hadn't heard anything…

"…? All of you! Do you not hear me? I'm offering you riches! Name your price!"

I guess they were going to let us get away with this. *Thank you, everyone!* Sometimes all good needed to triumph was for…well, for other good people to stand by and do nothing.

"Hey, Darkness. Remember when you stupidly tried to go beat the hydra by yourself, and how stupid that was? Well, running off to make a bride of yourself was even stupider, but all these people forgive you and are trying to help. Take a good look and see if you can get that through your rock-solid skull."

Happiness tinged Darkness's cheeks red; she looked down at the ground with just a hint of tears in her eyes.

What a happy ending. I decided not to ridicule Darkness any further, because I knew what those adventurers were thinking. All of them had big grins on their faces…

I had no doubt that for a long time, whenever Darkness showed up at the Guild, it was going to be, "Why, young Miss Lalatina! Aren't you going to wear one of your lovely dresses today?"

Everyone in town already knew that Darkness was actually the daughter of nobility. Axel's adventurers were shameless enough, and had known Darkness long enough, that I couldn't imagine they would treat her any differently at this point.

It was going to take a while for Darkness to live this one down, and I thought maybe I would keep my distance from her until she did.

…But as for the present moment? The guards outside the church, and the thugs inside it, had converged on us, resulting in something of a stalemate. These guys weren't idiots, and they weren't amateurs. They didn't look like they were going to do us the favor of being pushovers. On top of all that, they had numbers on their side. I didn't think we were going to get away without a fight.

I didn't want to pull a weapon; doing that right here in town would for sure make me a criminal. Of course, I sort of got the sense that I was already a criminal…

"Hrrgh…! Kazuma, my ability to hold back this magic is reaching its limit! Can I fire it already? Whatever we do, we're already lawbreakers! I'm ticked off, and I want to just drop an explosion on these clowns!"

Megumin's sudden outburst caused everyone around us to blanch. Me included, of course.

"Arrrgh! It's no good! I can't control it! Get away from me, everyone!"

No way! *This* was the moment when she lost control?!

If it had been anyone other than Megumin, I would have taken it for a bluff. But everyone there knew her too well. Faces pale, they all scrambled away. I made myself scarce, too, as—

"*Explosion*!!!"

* * *

Megumin let rip with a magical blast aimed straight at the sky. There was an immense noise and a blinding light above us. The shock wave shattered glass all over town and sent everyone in the vicinity diving for the ground, covering their ears.

"Now… Go now…" Aqua lifted up Megumin, who was drained of all her MP; for some reason, her voice trailed off, and finally she just fell silent and looked at me. Her cold stare eventually made me aware of my own situation. Specifically, the fact that I was currently crouched right behind Darkness, trying to stay hidden…

"Hey, Kazuma, hiding behind the person you're here to rescue is pretty low even for you," Aqua said.

"True," Megumin added. "I thought Kazuma looked awfully cool today, so cool that I was starting to worry I was seeing things. Thank goodness it was just my imagination."

"M-Mr. Kazuma… You're the worst…"

It was this last remark of Yunyun's that was hardest to bear.

For that matter, the other attendees were all looking at me from their places on the ground like I was human garbage.

But that wasn't important. What was important was that Megumin's explosion had shaken our opponents enough to give us a chance to escape. We broke through their blockade and set off running…or tried to.

"She can only use Explosion once per day! Get her! Get her now!"

I guess the shock just lasted a second, because the goons didn't show any hesitation this time.

Megumin shouted from Aqua's back, "Yunyun! I leave this to you—we will go on ahead! Whatever should happen to me, don't look back!"

"You moron!" Yunyun exclaimed. "We're friends now, aren't we? How could I ever leave you to— Hold on, what did you say? Megumin… Do you remember in Crimson Magic Village…? Doesn't this feel awfully familiar?!"

"I will trust you to buy us time, dear companion!" Megumin said. "Then from this day forth, I shall introduce you as my friend!"

"Fine, leave it to me! I'll do anything for a friend…!"

Yunyun seemed all too happy to run interference for us, and she gave our pursuers pause.

Dear, sweet Yunyun! I'd be your friend, if only you'd let me…!

We left her there and started running. Behind us, we heard someone shout, "She may be Crimson Magic Clan, but she's just one girl! Grab her before she finishes her spell!"

It was more than I could stand. Fine! I would stay behind, too, to give Darkness the chance to escape…!

I was just turning around when…

"Eeeyowch! He shoved me! Grr! My bones! It's breaking my bones! Dust, help meeeee!"

I heard a guy cry out and saw him rolling around on the floor.

"Hey, Keith, are you okay?! Yikes, that's nasty… I'm gonna knock you down and grind your bones to butter!"

That name… That voice… They sounded familiar.

"What's that?! I hardly touched him; why's he making such a racket? He's the one who threw himself at me! And then threw himself on the ground! If his bones are so broken, how is he holding on to my foot like that? Let go!"

That voice belonged to one of Alderp's goons.

I heard someone punkish behind us even as we ran. "Hey, hey, hey! Don't tell me you're gonna leave him paralyzed on the ground and try to run away without even saying you're sorry! I don't care if you work for the governor or God; you can't get away with that!"

The lackeys sounded more annoyed than anything else. "First his bones were broken; now he's paralyzed?! Forget it—you're in our way! Move! Get back or you'll regret it!"

I assumed that next, the goons tried to push the punk away.

"Eeeyowch! Here I was being all polite, and you had to go and get violent! You all saw it; he made the first move! Perfect, just what I wanted! Oh, you're gonna get it now! A certain noble gave me an awful lot of trouble just recently, and I didn't like nobles to begin with. You're the perfect way to work off a little steam!"

"Huh?! Hey, stop tha—!"

"Get him!"

"Get him! Get him!"

"Hey, let me have a piece of that!"

"I never did like that governor!"

"Ack! No! It's broken! I told you, it's broken!"

I took a glance back as we ran. The crowd of adventurers had turned Alderp's lackeys into punching bags. When all this had blown over, I would have to treat them to another round at the bar.

From what seemed like a great distance, I could hear a pained cry: "Lalatina! Don't go, Lalatina! Lalatinaaaaa!"

8

"Y-Young Lady?! What in the world happened to you? A-anyway, get inside!"

We had successfully escaped our pursuers and returned to Darkness's mansion. One of the guards hurriedly let us in. Between the fact that we had run out on the wedding ceremony and the tattered remains of Darkness's dress, everyone in the house was pretty shocked, but Darkness ignored them. She just started walking through the mansion.

The three of us followed her, not really sure where she was going.

Darkness ended up in front of one particular room.

"Father? I'm coming in."

Father? Ah. When I snuck into the house that one time, I'd shattered the window of his sickroom getting out. They must have moved him somewhere else.

Darkness didn't wait for an answer before entering. I thought maybe that was a little untoward for a noble maiden, but it turned out I was wrong: Her father was no longer in a state to answer her.

He was even thinner than he had been when I saw him last. There were dark bags under his eyes, and he was asleep, breathing deeply. The noise of our entry must have awakened him, because his eyes fluttered open.

One by one, Darkness and then the rest of us came to his bedside.

When he saw his daughter, he said, "...Ah...Lalatina. You look so beautiful. Just like your mother..." Then he smiled, kind but weak.

Darkness hid her face, unable to meet his gaze. "...Honored Father... I can only apologize to you. I know I was the one who pushed to go ahead with this wedding, but...I've broken the engagement, in the most humiliating way possible."

At that, her father's eyes crinkled in real happiness. "Is that so?! I'm so glad. You have nothing to worry about and nothing to apologize for." Then he turned to me. "Young Kazuma. Could you come here for a moment?"

I took a step closer to the bed.

Sensing the mood in the room, Megumin said, "...I believe I'll step out for some fresh air," and went into the hallway.

My *other* party member, on the other hand, who couldn't sense a mood to save her life, also stepped up to the bedside. I decided to let it go; even by my standards, it would be brutish to yell at someone right in front of a sick person.

Darkness's dad looked me in the face and smiled broadly. "...You've done well. Thank you. You have my gratitude."

All this thankfulness seemed a little sudden. "Me, sir? I only repaid my debt to your daughter."

That merely caused his smile to widen. Then he had to go and say something completely outrageous, considering Darkness was there and all.

"Young Kazuma. Please take my daughter for yourself. Please be so kind."

"Huh?!" Darkness said, shocked.

"Forget it! What kind of twisted game is this?"

"*Huh?!*" Darkness said, even more shocked. Then she looked at me as if she was about to shoot something back, but she didn't immediately say anything.

Her father watched us with palpable amusement.

...Crap. How had I gotten myself into this mess? The kingdom's confidant had apparently seen right through me.

Fine. If she has to go to somebody weird... Well, I'll look after her.

As if he had read my thoughts, Darkness's father's face relaxed and he exhaled.

...It didn't look like he had much time left.

He closed his eyes and whispered, "Lalatina. Do you enjoy the life you've been leading? So much that you could throw everything away for it?"

Darkness answered without a moment's hesitation. "I've loved it. I would give up everything I have to protect my friends."

Her father nodded once, as if satisfied to hear this, then murmured, "I see" very softly.

"Lalatina," he went on. "You must take the path you desire in life. Leave all the rest to me. I'm sure I have the strength left to write one last letter."

Darkness leaned in toward her father, took his hand.

"I love you, Father. Thank you for spending all these years raising me... Someday, when you're better, tell me stories of my dearly departed mother until I fall asleep, like you used to..."

"I love you, too, my sweet daughter. Yes, I'll be happy to tell you all about your mother, whom you so loved..."

Darkness's eyes brimmed.

"Yes... Sometime...," her father whispered, and then with a blissful smile he squeezed his daughter's hand.

Suddenly, a magic circle surrounded him and his whole bed.

"*Sacred Dispel*!"

The incantation came from the one person in the room who had a special gift for spoiling the moment.

"Ahhh!"

"F-Father?!"

Father and daughter both cried out at the sudden burst of light. When the flash faded, the bags had vanished from under his eyes, and although he was still thin, his skin had regained a certain glow.

............Um.

As we all stood staring, Aqua, sounding altogether too pleased with herself, exclaimed, "It was a curse! The old guy had a curse put on him by a pretty powerful demon. But it was no match for *my* strength!"

Darkness's dad lay healed by the power of this oblivious goddess, still holding his daughter's hand. They looked at each other.

"".........."""

Slowly, Darkness pulled her hand away. She glanced out the window, red up to her ears. Her father drew up his blanket, hiding his face in embarrassment. The little bit of his cheeks that I could see poking out from under the covers was bright red.

...Like father, like daughter.

"Now everything's fine! Yay, Darkness! Now your dad can tell you about your mom anytime!"

Aqua was genuinely thrilled. There was no malice in her at all.

Darkness, however, covered her face and slumped to her knees.

What a happy ending...

Interlude — Demons Cackle in the Night

"Arrrgh! Damn! Damn! Damn!"

I was in a secret underground room beneath my bedchamber, beating the daylights out of a cringing, grimy demon. Namely, Max, an incompetent fiend who had failed to grant even one of my wishes. I kicked him again and again.

"Wheeze... Wheeze... Wheeze..."

He made the strangest sound as he lay there, curled in a ball and covering his face. I kicked him again.

How long had it been since I had used that divine item to summon this low-level creature of darkness? Normally one comes to have *some* kind of affection for anybody one has known as long as this, but in this particular case, I had never been able to muster the slightest attachment no matter how much time passed.

"You! Miserable creature! If you were even slightly more useful, Lalatina would be mine now! Are you that inconsistent?! Are you that incoherent?! Worthless! Worthless! Worthless beast!"

"*Wheeze! Wheeze! Wheeze!* A demon is less powerful in a church building. More to the point, Alderp, it seems someone has broken the curse." He didn't even bother to uncurl himself as he delivered this devastating news.

"Broken the curse?! You! You can't even curse one wretched human to death?!" I resumed beating the demon mercilessly.

Why did I keep him around? Because his memory was so poor that he quickly forgot even whether he had received payment or not, which meant my expenses were minimal. But maybe it was time to think about cutting him loose.

And yet I would need his power again to cover up what had happened this time. Even I knew that the way I had spoken to Lalatina was inappropriate in front of all those nobles and powerful people. I let the blood go to my head and spoke violently to her in public, even though her house is of a far higher status than mine.

There was a silver lining, though. After the way that obnoxious little boy disrupted the wedding ceremony, I had every reason and every right to put him to death. Perhaps Lalatina would even offer herself to me in hopes of saving him.

"Max! By tomorrow morning, I want everyone who was at that church and everyone who might have heard what I said to have their memories altered! Make them think I was more…friendly. You have your orders!"

My thoughts turned to the coming day, and I made to leave the dank underground room, but then I heard Max's voice behind me.

"*Wheeze… Wheeze…* That's impossible, Alderp. I lack…the power."

I stopped in my tracks. *Impossible?*

Max might have been worthless, but in all our time together, he had never once spoken back to me. No matter what I asked him to do, no matter how much he was to alter the facts, he had never deemed a request of mine impossible. Why now?

"Impossible, you say? I know better than anyone that you're a low-level demon. This divine item summoned you at random, after all. But still, you have no right to refuse me. So do it! I don't care if it's impossible; just do the job! Are you worried there's too many? Memory alteration is your specialty! Do it!"

And yet…

"It's impossible. The light… *Wheeze.* The light that broke the curse is too strong; it keeps me at bay. It makes the task impossible."

Now I was well and truly angry. "Fine, you incompetent fool! I'll tear up our contract and get some other, better demon! This is my final order to you: Bring Lalatina… Use your powers to compel her to appear before me immediately. Then I will pay you what is owed!"

That got Max's attention. "Pay me? You'll pay me my due?"

"Yes. I mean it. Your own idiocy has caused you to forget that I've already paid you several times. But this time I'll pay you for real. Now! Bring Lalatina to me!" It was so kind of me to clue in this hopelessly forgetful monster.

…That was when I heard it: a knock on the door of my basement room, a room no one else should have known about.

"Lord Governor, are you there? It's me. I've come to apologize for today. Won't you come out?"

What was she doing here at this hour? How did she know about this room? But never mind all that! Because that voice was one I could never mistake…!

"Lalatina! You've come, Lalatina! G-good! Excellent work, Max! I praise you, I truly do! I have no idea what you did, but I'll pay you, just as I promised. And our contract is finished! I set you free! Ahh, Lalatina, I'm coming!"

"And I haven't even done anything! *Wheeze, wheeze!* You'll pay me? And end our contract?"

Max was muttering something to himself, but I ignored him, rushing to the door of the room. I could see Lalatina looking down at me. And what a seductive negligee she was in! She smiled with an affection I had never seen from her before and came down the stairs into the room.

That smile—that *body*—I was immediately possessed by the most hideous lust.

Looking apologetic, Lalatina murmured sweetly, "I'm very sorry, milord. Let me apologize for what happened today. Please, just…take my body and spare my friends!"

Suddenly I understood it all. Just as I had expected, she had come to beg me for mercy.

I could be patient no longer. How many years had I wished for this girl, and now here she was before me—and in such a state!

I couldn't even wait for her to get down the stairs. I threw myself at her—

And then Lalatina smirked, and her body began to twist and distort.

"Bwa-ha-ha-ha-ha! Did you think it was Lalatina? Too bad—it is I! Ahh! Now, *that* is negativity! Delicious! Exquisite! Bwa-ha-ha-ha-ha-ha!"

A masked man was standing there, wearing a tuxedo just like Max's.

"Wha—?! Wh-who the hell are you? Why am I shivering? You give off the same aura as Max! You're a demon! You are, aren't you?!" I pointed an accusatory finger at him.

The masked demon grinned.

"Max! Kill this filthy servant of evil!" I shouted, pointing at the newcomer. I ground my teeth in frustration at being duped. How dare he turn into my Lalatina, the one I'd so long desired!

My disappointment was absolute. Never, never would I forgive this!

"…? Why should I kill my fellow? *Wheeze…?* Hmm? Say…have we met before?"

He showed no sign of listening to my orders. Had sass become his new normal? What was wrong with him today? Had he, at last, truly broken?

As these thoughts ran through my mind, the masked demon before me gave a bow of such perfection that any nobleman would have envied it.

"How many hundreds or thousands of times have I introduced myself to you? Well, once again—it is a pleasure to meet you, Maxwell. Maxwell the Adjuster. He who can change the facts. I am the all-seeing demon Vanir. Maxwell, demon who can bend the truth, I have come for you!"

He calls this incompetent creature not Max but Maxwell? Wait… What does he mean, come for him?

"Vanir! Vanir! For some reason I feel…I feel you're very familiar! We must have met before. Haven't we met before?"

"Bwa-ha-ha-ha-ha-ha! You say the same thing every time! Your name is Maxwell! You are my fellow, who has come here from another world without his memories! Now, let us return to Hell, where you belong!"

"W-wait just one moment!" I exclaimed. "He is my slave! You can't just take him from me!"

This caused the demon called Vanir to laugh. "Slave? Maxwell, a Duke of Hell just as I am—your slave? O greedy man, who has nothing in abundance but ill luck. For once, luck was with you. It was your good fortune that Maxwell happened to be the first demon you summoned. Any other demon might well have ripped you apart the instant he appeared, without any talk of 'pay'! But you were lucky! Maxwell understands nothing! He is powerful yet no more thoughtful than a babe. He raised you to the position you now have, and you would do well to be very, very grateful."

I couldn't comprehend what he was saying. My pet, Max, a Duke of Hell? And what did he mean about my status? I had gotten where I was under my own power. That shattered husk of a demon was hardly a toy in comparison.

My confusion only caused Vanir to smile wider. "And as I recall, when I appeared, you told Maxwell that you would pay him what he was owed, that your contract was over, and that he was free."

Damn it all! He was right about that anyway. When I said those things, I had been under the mistaken impression that it was Max's power that had brought Lalatina to me. In my elation, I had forgotten myself and allowed myself to say those foolish things.

Hadn't this creature called himself the all-seeing demon? In other words, he had arrived here at this precise moment, knowing that this would happen.

As if he had read my very thoughts, the demon said, "Yes, your contract with Maxwell was something of a problem. Goodness, but I've had to take a roundabout route!"

Roundabout? "Wh-why, you—! You don't mean *you*—?!"

"Indeed! It's precisely as you imagine! It was I who enabled that boy to repay the debt and I who told him about you. Bwa-ha-ha-ha-ha! Good, very good! An exceptional animosity! A veritable delicacy!"

Clenching my shaking fist, I said, "What a damnable ruse! What a thing to do...! If you wanted this broken-down excuse for a demon, you should have said so! If you had told me what the both of you were to begin with, I would have given him to you immediately! There was no need to stir up the entire town, humiliate me in public—!"

Yes! Had I known that an omniscient demon was running around my town, I would never have been so bold...

What the demon said to me in response was simple, straightforward, and unbelievably stupid.

"This way was more fun! Bwa-ha-ha-ha-ha, what a sight it was to see! Even that goddess danced to my tune this time! While that thuggish little deity was at the ceremony, she even had to submit to the humiliation of having *me* tend her egg! Mm, such terrible negativity! And then there's the hatefulness of a man who has loved and lusted for so long, and then—then, just as his perverse desires were about to bear fruit, just as he was about to gain what he had so long sought, his bride was snatched away from him! I find that if I were destroyed at this very moment, I could die a happy demon!"

Just what in the hell is this creature babbling about?!

"Now then, Lord Governor. I have no further business with you. I shall escort Maxwell back to Hell and then return to labor away under that ridiculous shopkeeper."

It seemed the demon intended to go home, wherever that was. Very well. I hadn't realized Max was so powerful, but I would get along fine without him.

But what was I going to do about tomorrow? It was too late now to erase the evidence of what I had done. But just as I was worrying about that, I heard Max huffing excitedly.

"*Wheeze! Wheeze!* Vanir! Vanir! Before we go home, I must receive my payment from Alderp! He told me! He said he would pay what was owed!"

Damn! I did say that, didn't I…?

"Fine, fine, your payment. Take your payment and—"

—go home, I was about to say, when a muffled crunch echoed through the dark basement room. It took me a moment to register that it was the sound of my own arms breaking.

"…Hr—arrgh! Arrrrrggggghhhhhh!"

Max was standing there, observing his handiwork.

My breath came in ragged gasps. "Hhh! It h— It hurts!" I cried as he dragged me up by my broken limbs.

"Alderp! Alderp! What a fine sound you make! *Wheeze! Wheeze!*"

What foolishness was my broken demon talking now?

"What is this?! Max, let me go! Stop! Stop that, owwwww!"

My weeping and yelling elicited an expression from the demon, the first I had seen in all the time I'd known him. His impassive, mask-like face twisted horrifically, and he laughed as if he was truly enjoying himself.

At that, Vanir burst out laughing. "Bwa-ha-ha-ha! Maxwell, why not continue this when we get back to Hell? This man owes you a very great deal. Bring him with us and extract your price slowly."

Even my pain-addled brain could detect the menace in those words.

"Under the terms of the contract by which you employed Maxwell, payment is to be granted in the form of his favorite flavor of negativity for a set period of time," Vanir said. "Hmm, interesting. You've led a most indulgent life and mistreated Maxwell rather spectacularly… I highly doubt you can pay all you owe even if you devote the rest of your life to the effort…"

The masked demon's words sent a freezing chill down my spine. I nearly forgot about the pain in my arms as my body began to shake, and I stared desperately at the monster.

"V-very well! I was wrong to be so cruel! I have a proposition. First, take my—"

"Enormous wealth? Once Maxwell returns to Hell, your various misdeeds shall come to light, and you shall have no wealth at all. Everything shall be given into the care of the Dustiness family... It shall be distributed to that boy—the one who is just now at home, thinking that perhaps he shouldn't have used all his money to save that girl and that maybe he'll make her repay him with her body—along with the town and the nation. I, Vanir, the all-seeing demon, declare: From this moment forth, you are penniless."

I gnashed my teeth at that, nearly frothing at the mouth. All my hard-earned treasure...!

"In—"

"In that case, take any number of servants from your house in your own place? Such a shame! The burden of payment falls only upon the one who entered into the contract. Ah! A fine fit of dark emotion, but that despair you're feeling isn't the flavor I prefer. It's more to Maxwell's liking."

At that, my body finally refused to stop shaking.

"M-Ma— M-M-Max! Max...! I—I ad-m-mit, I did some unconscionable things to you... Terrible things. I beg of you: Won't you save me? Won't you forgive me? I know how it seemed, but I never hated you! It's true! I beg of you, Max!"

Vanir continued to grin broadly as I spoke, but for whatever reason, he made no move to correct my lies.

I felt Max let go of my arms. I collapsed to the floor.

The faintest flicker of hope entered my heart; I looked up at Max fearfully.

He was smiling merrily...and with unutterable cruelty. This demon, who had remained expressionless the entire time we had known each other, now wore the innocent smile of a child.

"Alderp! Alderp! Me too! I love you, too, Alderp!"

Vanir was still grinning. What did he think was so funny about this?

The broken demon I had known so long, the smile now covering his entire face, went on. "Alderp! Alderp! I love you, too, Alderp! When we get back to Hell, I shall always be with you, Alderp! Always, always feasting on your despair!"

Now I saw it. Now I saw why I had never been able to feel anything for this creature.

Deep inside, I must have been afraid of his true nature. And now, with him smiling down at me, I was utterly terrified.

Oh gods.... Please...

"Ho! How good to know your affection is mutual, Alderp," Vanir interjected. "You'll be glad to know, Maxwell is a very dedicated demon. I'm sure he'll *attend* to you every hour of every day! Bwa-ha-ha-ha-ha-ha-ha! Bwa-ha-ha-ha-ha-ha-ha!"

My one lone hope was that this monster would soon tire of "attending" to me and grant me an easy death...

Listening to that masked demon cackle, for the first time in my life, I prayed to the gods.

"I'll take good care of you, Alderp! Unlike you, who are content to have your way with the girls you abduct and then simply cast them aside, I'll take extra care to be sure I don't use you up—ever! *Wheeze, wheeze! Wheeze, wheeze!!*"

Epilogue 1 — Welcome Home!

It was the morning of the day after we had absconded from the church with Darkness.

"That lord went missing?"

Darkness came by the mansion as soon as the sun was up, and I could hardly believe what she told me. Why would that old bastard, who wouldn't shut up about his "Lalatina! Lalatinaaaa!" suddenly just disappear?

"His household staff swear they searched everywhere, but they couldn't find a trace of him," Darkness said.

I looked at her, puzzled. I had been sure the old man's personal army was going to show up at my door this morning.

"Plus, for some reason, people have been discovering likely evidence of his wrongdoings all morning. It looks like he was even the one who sent that body-swapping divine item to Princess Iris. People are speculating that he ran off somewhere when he realized he couldn't hide the evidence anymore."

That makes sense…

"…Meaning *you* won't need to flee in the middle of the night, so put those things down," Darkness said with some exasperation.

I set down the luggage I had strapped to my back. Behind me, Megumin and Aqua did the same. We had been getting ready to go to ground in some distant field for a while until things cooled off here.

"Well, that's good, I guess. Anyway, what are you doing out there, Darkness? Hurry up and come inside." She was standing just beyond the front door, making no move to come in.

Darkness, however, did nothing of the sort; she only stood there looking troubled.

"What's wrong, Darkness? Is anything the matter?" Megumin asked.

"Oh!" Aqua exclaimed. "I get it! Megumin, you got to the ceremony late, so you don't know! Just listen to this! Darkness ended up getting *bought* by Kazuma! He paid off her entire debt. He was all, *You belong to me now!* and *I'm gonna make you pay me back with your body!* Darkness doesn't want to come inside because she's afraid of what Kazuma might do to her. Aren't you, Darkness?"

"...Huh?"

"H-hey, let's talk this out. You've got this all wrong. Well, not *wrong* exactly, but—not right, either! I don't like the way you told that story!"

Megumin's red eyes were flashing, and she was looking at me the way one might look at a bit of dirt.

Darkness, however, shook her head. "...No, that's not it. It's true, Kazuma told me in front of all those people to pay with my body and called me a perverted Crusader..."

Erk... Megumin was starting to chant her magic...

But then Darkness abruptly bowed her head. "I'm sorry. I acted selfishly and caused problems for all of you as a result. Even I know I was an idiot this time. Please, forgive me...!"

Aqua and Megumin hurried over to Darkness.

"It's all right! You came back to us, and that's what matters. As far as I'm concerned, it's water under the bridge. Kazuma may have lost most of his net worth, but he'll stop working the moment he gets a bit of pocket money. All's well that ends well," Megumin said.

"That's right," Aqua added. "In fact, if this hadn't happened, I would never have gone to your house. And then we would never have known about the curse on your dad! …Hey, we have to find out who cursed him to begin with! Personally, I suspect that masked demon did it. In fact, with my unclouded vision, I'm certain of it! We should go *thank* him…!"

The two girls showered Darkness with reassurances, but she was looking straight at me.

"I owe you a great debt, Kazuma," she said. "You said you gave up everything to get that money. I can't promise it will happen immediately, but I'll arrange for the state to compensate you for what you paid. When my father is fully recovered, I expect you'll be repaid out of the assets reclaimed from Alderp. However…" Her face clouded. "…We won't be able to get back the intellectual property rights you sold. I know you were intending to live a safe life as a businessman, but…"

Was that what she was worried about?

"What, that?" I said. "Forget about it. I have the Cooking skill, so I can open a street stall or something. Make food from my home country, save up a little change… Hey, hold on a second. I'm going to get my money back?" Now she had my complete attention.

"Yes, you will. All two billion eris you spent on my behalf. As well as the compensation for the lord's mansion and the money for the destroyed buildings. You incurred those debts protecting this town, after all. The lord should have disbursed the money to the people." She paused. "But now that I think about it… Why did I accept his excuses so readily? Why did I just pay him the money? It's almost like I was… hypnotized or something. And why has all the evidence of his crimes come to light so suddenly…?"

She couldn't quite seem to figure it out. But who cared?

Who cared?!

"T-two *billion*…?"

Hip hip hooray! I would never have to work another day in my life!

Wait… Hang on just one second. There's twenty-four hours in a day. And *that* service runs five thousand eris for three hours. With two billion eris, I could just live in my own personal dream world for the rest of my life…

As I stood there imagining the possibilities, Megumin and Aqua closed in on me.

"Say, Kazuma," Aqua began, "you're looking very— Yes! Exceedingly heroic today. So cool. Ahem, Kazuma, Emperor Zel needs a top-quality house to live in!"

"Indeed, very heroic and cool. You know I've always thought you were cool, Kazuma. On that note, I would love a magical item that increases the destructive power of my spells."

"Hey! You money-grubbing— You get one whiff of cash and look what happens…! Darkness, what's wrong?" She was watching the three of us, but she still hadn't moved from her place near the front door.

"Geez, come on already," I said. "So you've been secretly cleaning up our messes, right? I know that yesterday I got all angry about you doing that without ever telling me, but the truth is, it made me a little happy, too. And now I've repaid that debt. Plus, I'm going to get all my money back. So it's basically as if nothing at all happened yesterday, right?"

Frankly, with the amount of money that was coming to me, I could overlook a lot of little things. Given how much I had been cooped up in the house lately, I was ready to rent the best room in town; schedule some sweet, sweet dreams; and get out of here for about a week.

Darkness, however, seemed bothered when I mentioned "nothing at all."

"Does that mean… You take back saying you bought me, too?"

Aqua and Megumin, who had been cozied up trying to get some cash, were suddenly glaring at me from inches away.

… C-c'mon, stop that.

"Sure, strike it! Let's all agree to forget everything that happened yesterday!"

But that just made Darkness look even more depressed.

...Huh? Was there a chance she had actually *wanted* to belong to me? Was this some kind of twisted reverse confession of love?

She seemed to have something else in mind, though (sadly). Looking at the ground, nearly crying, Darkness said, "About... About that letter I wrote. The one asking you guys to count me out of your party..."

Ah. So that was it. She still felt she had removed herself from our group. And if we said yesterday hadn't happened, that would mean I never made that remark about her paying me back with her body as a Crusader...

So much for my hopes of a confession.

"What are you saying? You are our precious Crusader, Darkness. How could we ever let you go?" Megumin asked.

"She's right, what a ridiculous thing to worry about. You sure can be dumb sometimes, Darkness. Anyway, where else would you go?" Aqua added.

...Shoot. They beat me to the punch.

Darkness laced her fingers in front of her chest and looked at me, distinctly uneasy. I guess she couldn't relax until she heard it directly from me.

But just as I was about to open my mouth, Darkness burst out, "I-I'm a—! I'm a poor excuse for a Crusader! My attacks never hit, and my toughness is my only redeeming quality! B-but do you think...? Could you find it in your heart to let me join this party again?"

I gave the stuttering, nervous Darkness a rueful smile. "How could I not?" I said. "Welcome home."

"I-I'm home!" Darkness exclaimed.

Tears filled her eyes, a relieved smile blossomed on her face, and—

"Hey, Kazuma. Aren't you a little disappointed by the way this turned out? When you said Darkness would have to repay you with her body, are you sure you didn't have at least a little bit of naughtiness in mind?"

Aqua, whose only distinguishing trait seemed to be her inability to read a mood, had a hand to her mouth, covering a big grin.

...What in the hell was she on about?

"Come to think of it, he announced Darkness was his property in front of all those people. What was that supposed to be? Some kind of declaration of love? Remember when Yunyun suggested they should have kids? And how easily he got close to Iris in the capital? And now this. How easily his affections change! He tried to get his hands on me when we were sleeping together at Crimson Magic Village—but look how fickle he turns out to be. You need to pull yourself together."

Even Megumin was getting in on it, looking a bit put out. What was *she* blathering about now? What was she, jealous? *Do us all a favor and be clear yourself.* I wished they would all be more obvious. Easy-to-understand, one-note characters like in a harem anime.

That was when I noticed that Darkness looked...strange. She didn't look fidgety and scared anymore; instead, she was stealing these little glances at Megumin and me as we stood fighting like an old married couple.

"...N-now that you mention it, when Kazuma broke into my house the other day, we very nearly crossed the final frontier..."

"""Whaaaat?!"""

Why would she say something like that when she was so obviously embarrassed about it? Aqua and Megumin were both shocked.

"H-hey, stop that...," I said weakly. "Seriously, stop. I mean...we *didn't*, did we? In the end?"

"""You mean you *almost did*?!""" Aqua and Megumin exclaimed.

I was just digging my own grave here...

"Hey, Kazuma, just how much of an idiot are you? What were you *doing* while Megumin and I were working so hard to get Darkness back?"

"Kazuma, do you mean to say you didn't go to bring her back at all but to have yourself a little tryst?! Just when I think my opinion of you can't get any lower! What in the world did you do?!"

Hey, hold on. It was one thing when I played my little joke on Megu-

min back at Crimson Magic Village, but this time I didn't do anything wrong!

Darkness, sounding a little bashful, said, "*Tryst* is such a strong word. All he did was force his way into my room in the middle of the night, cover my mouth before I could scream, shove me onto the bed, hold me down while I struggled...and then touch my stomach as I lay there fighting and nearly naked. But that's it!"

""Wha—?!""

"Wait just a dang second! I mean—that's true! That's all true, but—!"

"""?!"""

Megumin and Aqua backed away from me.

"It's never been any secret that you had a sexual interest in Darkness, but I never imagined you were the type to just cop a feel the moment you got a chance," Megumin said. "I believed you were a terrible but surprisingly loyal and sometimes upright person. So what about when we were together? You didn't have any interest in me, did you? You just wanted to do it! As long as a woman was sleeping next to you, you wouldn't care who she was!"

I wished she would take a breath. Otherwise it seemed like she wasn't going to stop talking until my reputation was completely in tatters. But as I tried to break in enough to defend myself, Aqua joined the attack.

"No kidding! Back when Kazuma and I were still sleeping in the stable together, this animal kept watching like a hawk for any opportunity to take advantage of me!"

"Now, *that* is categorically not true."

"Why *not*?!"

Aqua was weeping and trying to strangle me. I put a hand against her face to hold her back. Darkness, embarrassed though she was, couldn't avoid a hint of a triumphant smirk. Apparently, this was her way of getting me back for impersonating her the night I broke in.

Her arms were crossed and she seemed to enjoy seeing me beset by my accusers. There was only one thing to say…

"*You* were the one who suggested we 'become adults together…'"

I didn't even shout it; I just muttered.

"""!!"""

"I d-d-d-d-did not! I just figured, since I was going to be that lord's wife anyway, there was no reason not to—"

"She admitted it!" Aqua exclaimed. "Darkness admitted that she was the one who started it! Goodness gracious me! …Welp, I think the polite thing would be to make myself scarce. I'm going to take Emperor Zel's egg to the park for some sunbathing."

"Darkness! I am shocked to discover what a slut you are! You play the tragic heroine but secretly crave sex… It was my mistake to worry about you!"

"Wait just a— N-no, no, really, wait! Waaaaiiit!"

Darkness, the end of Megumin's staff shoved uncomfortably against her cheek, gave me a withering look. Apparently, she wasn't through yet.

I grabbed Aqua before she could head out the door with her precious egg. Then I said the thing that I hadn't intended to reveal until Darkness had calmed down a bit.

"…Say, Aqua. I've been wondering. How's marriage work around here? Who joins whose family?"

To the untrained ear, it sounded like I was launching into a completely new subject.

"Well, that's all very sudden, Kazuma," Aqua said. "On the morning of the day of the ceremony, you submit some paperwork to the city hall affirming that you've become man and wife. And then in the afternoon, you have…the…ceremony…"

She seemed to realize what I was saying. So did Megumin, who suddenly looked very disturbed.

"…? What's going on?" Only the sheltered noblewoman remained oblivious.

Megumin, as if to play along, said, "I—I guess divorcées aren't so rare nowadays… Yes, it'll be fine!"

At last, Darkness put two and two together, and she looked up with a start.

She was nobility but also a total perverted masochist; she was a virgin and yet also divorced. How many layers did she think she could pile on, here?

"Wait… So… What happens now? Darkness was abducted halfway through the ceremony. And her husband ran away that very night. I guess everyone will assume he got rid of her." Aqua's words, guileless as ever, caused Darkness to tremble.

She looked me full in the face, hesitant, anxious…

"Well, we can pretend the paperwork doesn't exist, so don't worry about it…………Divorce-ness."

Darkness spun on her heel and dashed off, crying.

Epilogue 2 — Eris and Chris

"And that's pretty much the story. Darkness hasn't come out of her house since then. I'm planning another break-in…"

I was in a cozy little café on the outskirts of town. A bit of a hole-in-the-wall. We were the only ones there.

"Well, it sounds like you're as much of a monster as you ever were. Don't be too hard on Darkness, okay? She may look tough, but she's really pretty sensitive."

"Yeah, yeah, I know. What about you, Chris? What have you been up to all this time? How long does it take to get to Axel from the Capital?"

Chris had finally gotten back from the royal city, and I was bringing her up to speed on recent events. She scratched the scar on her cheek in embarrassment. "Aww, y'know. I've been busy. I was actually just nearby once, but then I was called away all of a sudden. I had to take care of some stuff before I could finally get back here." She stretched out over the table, exhausted.

"Called away? Who could call you? Is there some kind of guild for thieves?"

"Er… Well, you know how it is. When someone dies, things just get…"

"Don't tell me you moonlight as an undertaker."

Chris didn't dignify that with a response but only sighed deeply. "Can you believe it?" she said. "That divine item we were looking for—all this time that lord had it. When I broke into his home in the capital, I just assumed I had made a mistake because of Miss Aqua's divine item!"

I'd heard that the second divine item Chris and I had been looking for in the capital had turned up in Alderp's basement. Chris had gone to collect it first thing when she got back to town. Supposedly, the item allowed you to control a randomly summoned monster. I wondered what the old fart had planned to do with something like that.

By the time I finished explaining everything, Chris's coffee had gone cold. She drained her cup in a single gulp, then said, "Anyway, all's well that ends well. Thanks for helping Darkness out, Lowly Assistant."

"Sure thing, Chief." We both smiled.

"*Sigh*… I still haven't gotten back that other item, though. Hey, Lowly Assistant, would you—?"

"I'm telling you right now, I'm busy."

Chris puffed out her cheeks, annoyed that I hadn't let her finish. "I'd pay you…"

"I've got plenty of money."

Chris scratched at her scar again, in consternation this time. "Pfah. Fine. You're on notice—I'll get you to help me again soon." Then a gentle smile came over her face.

……Huh?

That smile, combined with the way she scratched her cheek… Something felt off. Or…like I'd seen them somewhere recently.

You know, I'd been wondering: Why would Chris talk about "Darkness" and "Megumin" but go out of her way to refer to "Miss Aqua"?

And then there was the fact that even her name sounded a bit like someone else I knew… Someone with the same color hair and even the same color eyes.

That person called Aqua her "senior" and talked about "Miss Megumin."

But she still just called Darkness "Darkness."

Could it be because Darkness was her…friend?

I had the urge for a little mischief.

Chris was just getting up and waving good-bye when I said:

"By the way, Lady Eris. Where are you keeping the divine item you took back from His Lordship?"

"Oh, that? I sealed it up in the cave where the hydra used to—"

Chris—or rather, the goddess Eris—stopped where she was, that same sweet smile frozen on her face.

Afterword

Natsume Akatsuki here, light-novel author and capable of telling one baby chick from another.

An anime.

We're getting an anime!

On that note, I'd like to let you know about this, that, and the other thing, but I'll have to ask you to check The Sneaker WEB website for details.

I swear I'm not just being lazy; they give me only so much space for these afterwords! I have other priorities for these pages. Please forgive me!

On that note, I have a very important announcement.

Behold: I have received *four whole fan letters*! Yahoo!

Now, now, I know what you're thinking: *Why would he go out of his way to mention that? Ugh!* But it's just that it's easy for me to count them because I store each one neatly and carefully.

I suspect—indeed, am convinced and fully believe—that the majority of authors obsessively store their fan mail and then sit there smiling at it.

I must admit, to my embarrassment, that I haven't yet answered any of them.

There's a reason, though. I'm supposedly a professional writer, yet my handwriting is way worse than the stuff in these letters. Please just hang on until I clean it up a little bit. I'm reading a famous manga featuring a calligrapher as a main character, so I'm sure I'll get it soon.

I know what you're thinking: This *is what he was so eager to talk about? What about that other stuff?* Okay, I'll throw you a bone.

I just recently became Natsume of Saitama!

What I mean is, I moved house.

I promise it isn't because my parents chased me out, telling me that since I had a real job, it was time to give up my life as a residential security guard and get out of the house. I use the word *moved*, but it's only temporary; I fully intend to land back at my family home and resume my shut-in status.

You're probably getting angry about now (*he skipped telling us about the anime to write this inane crap?*), so let me append a proper announcement.

A new spin-off, separate from *May There Be an Explosion on this Wonderful World!*, is going to be serialized briefly on The Sneaker WEB. The main character will be a certain assistant to a certain unprofitable shopkeeper.

As for the plot, it will feature townspeople, each of whom naturally has one or two little quirks, coming to this character for advice. A lonely girl makes a bad choice of friends; a certain princess, influenced by one NEET's tall tales (all taken from *Mito Komon*), gets the idea to imitate her hero... In short, it lets us focus on characters who don't normally get to stand in the spotlight. I hope you'll give it a look.

Okay, then. Once again I owe a profound debt to Kurone Mishimasensei, my editor, and all the many other people without whom this book would not have seen publication.

But especially to you, dear reader.

You have my deepest thanks!

Natsume Akatsuki

AFTERWORD!
An anime! Congrats!
Hooraaaaay
Here's a smiling Aqua-sama!
2015.9
Kurone Mishima

CONGRATULATIONS ON REACHING SEVEN VOLUMES AND GETTING AN ANIME! I'LL START WAITING ANXIOUSLY FOR THE BROADCAST RIGHT NOW!
Hope you'll check out the manga version, too!
MASAHITO WATARI

NEXT
Hey, just a second! Apparently, there's going to be a festival of gratitude to Eris—totally ignoring the fact that I'm her senior goddess! Well, that does it! I'm going to show those Eris pip-squeaks the power of the Axis Church!
You'll all help me, won't you?
?!
I don't know what you have planned, but I know someone who owes a lot to the Axis Church. Very well.
?!?!
As a d-devout Eris follower, I'm not sure I can...
Phew...
Darkness, how could you? Fine, I'll get Chris to help me instead!
?!?!?!
Next time, Axis Church vs. Eris Sect!
Lowly Assistant?!
KONOSUBA: GOD'S BLESSING ON THIS WONDERFUL WORLD! 8
Axis Church vs. Eris Sect
COMING SOON!!

Read the light novel that inspired the hit anime series!
Re:ZeRo
-Starting Life in Another World-
Re:ZeRo
-Starting Life in Another World-
TAPPEI NAGATSUKI
ILLUSTRATION BY SHINICHIROU OTSUKA
Re:ZeRo
-Starting Life in Another World-
TAPPEI NAGATSUKI
ILLUSTRATION BY SHINICHIROU OTSUKA
ART: DAICHI MATSUSE
ORIGINAL STORY: TAPPEI NAGATSUKI
CHARACTER DESIGN: SHINICHIROU OTSUKA
Re:ZeRo
-Starting Life in Another World-
Chapter 1: A Day in the Capital
ART: DAICHI MATSUSE
Re:ZeRo
Also be sure to check out the manga series!
AVAILABLE NOW!
Yen Press
YEN ON
www.YenPress.com
Re:Zero Kara Hajimeru Isekai Seikatsu
© Tappei Nagatsuki, Daichi Matsuse / KADOKAWA CORPORATION
© Tappei Nagatsuki Illustration: Shinichirou Otsuka/ KADOKAWA CORPORATION

Is it WRONG to TRY to PICK UP GIRLS IN A DUNGEON?
1
FUJINO OMORI
ILLUSTRATION BY SUZUHITO YASUDA

Another
yukito ayatsuji

1
KAZUMA KAMACHI
ILLUSTRATION BY
KIYOTAKA HAIMURA
A Certain Magical Index